# Jeff McLean:
## His Courtship

By
Mr. and Mrs. Stephen  B. Castleberry

Castleberry Farms Press

Distributed by
**THE COURTSHIP CONNECTION**
**P.O. BOX 424 TEMPERANCE, MI  48182**
(734) 847-5210 • E-Mail Kmorris895@aol.com
Call, Write, or E-Mail for a <u>Free</u> Catalog

First Edition
© Copyright 1998

Castleberry Farms Press
P.O. Box 337
Poplar, WI 54864

Printed in the U.S.A.

Cover art was created by:
Jeffrey T. Larson
11947 E. State Rd. 13
Maple, Wisconsin 54854
(715) 364-8473

# A Note From the Authors

We believe that the father should be the spiritual leader and teacher in the family, *not* this book. Many use our books as "read aloud" material for the entire family. We encourage you to do so, and challenge you to spend time discussing what you've read. Look up the Bible verses mentioned, talk about what the characters are thinking and doing, discuss what should have been done differently, etc. Such interaction will magnify the value of our humble work.

This book describes how one family followed courtship. There is not just *one* process or way in which courtship could work and we hope you won't base your courtship expectations solely on our book. Dear young readers, follow the leadership of your parents.

In the back of this book is information about the other titles we publish, including an order form. We always welcome your comments, suggestions, and most importantly, your prayers.

**Mr. and Mrs. Stephen B. Castleberry**
**P.O. Box 337**
**Poplar, WI 54864**

# Chapter One

J eff, run! Jump the fence! Get out of there!"

There was fear in Luke's voice. Jeff looked over his shoulder, and what he saw sent a chill down his back. An angry bull, easily weighing more than 2500 pounds, was charging directly toward him. This was truly a matter of life and death. Many farming communities have had someone killed by a bull, often a bull that the farmer mistakenly trusted as a gentle animal.

Jeff turned quickly to the left and raced for the fence. *Twenty-five feet away*, he thought. *Surely I can make it!* If he could only reach the fence, it would be easy to quickly climb over it to safety.

As he ran, he heard a terrific crash behind him. *Where's Luke?* he suddenly thought. *Is he back there getting hurt?* Looking back, he saw that Luke, his brother-in-law, was safely on the other side of the opposite fence. Jeff's sister Sarah was there too, her fearful eyes focused on Jeff. The bull had crashed into a temporary fence that was now nothing more than a pile of splintered boards. The bull, seemingly not fazed by the impact, had turned, and looking at Jeff, was beginning to paw at the ground.

"Run, Jeff!" Sarah screamed. "He's coming after you again!"

Safety was only a few feet away, but as Jeff took his next step, his right foot landed in a depression in the ground. It wasn't exactly a hole. It was just where the cows had walked during a rainy time last

9

spring and had left the ground pockmarked. It was deep enough, however, to cause Jeff to twist his ankle and fall momentarily to the ground. Pain. And nausea. He was up again in an instant, but now it was all he could do to walk toward the fence, limping heavily. Sarah screamed again.

There was some commotion behind Jeff, but he couldn't be concerned about that right now. He had to make it to the fence, and fast! In what seemed like forever, he finally reached the fence and painfully maneuvered himself to the other side. Looking back, he saw Luke climbing the opposite fence quickly with the bull right on his heels. Slumping to the ground, Jeff tried to figure it all out. *How did Luke get inside the fence? I thought he was safely on the other side.*

Soon Sarah and Luke were hovering over Jeff. "Are you all right?" Luke asked, panting as if he had just run a mile at top speed.

Sarah didn't wait for an answer and was already examining Jeff's ankle and leg. "I think it's just sprained," she told her brother. Then turning to Luke, she hugged him tightly, tears filling her eyes. "Luke, that was very dangerous. You could have been killed! I was so afraid." That was all she managed to say before she broke down in sobs.

"I thought you were outside the fence," Jeff mumbled to Luke. The nausea hadn't left and the pain was getting worse, making him feel confused.

Luke didn't say anything. He just hugged Sarah, his bride of two years.

By now, David McLean, Jeff's father, had reached them. After making sure Jeff was not seriously hurt, he addressed Luke. "That was a very brave thing you did, Luke," Mr. McLean said, giving Luke's arm a squeeze. After a minute, he added quietly, "Thank you."

"He would have done it for me," Luke said. "The Lord gave me the strength. I didn't know if I could make it or not. We need to thank Him."

Suddenly Jeff's mind cleared enough to realize that Luke had jumped into the pen to coax away the angry bull, saving Jeff's life. "Thank You, Lord," Jeff whispered. "And thank You for Luke," he added.

Jeff's mom was on the scene now, and quickly evaluated the situation. In no time, she had Jeff in the house with his leg propped up, a cold water bottle on the ankle, and had given him some strong herbs for the pain. Dad and Luke were talking about the accident.

"How do you suppose Giant got out?" Dad asked.

Luke, his son-in-law, answered. "I suppose he must have been pushing against that corral fence all morning and we just didn't notice it. We were so busy with the other animals that we didn't have time to check up on him. We had two young bulls in the group and I guess he felt they were too near his territory or something."

"I suppose so," Dad replied. "Well, I've got him shut back in his own paddock now, so we shouldn't have any more problems. I'm just thankful that no one got hurt badly, or worse . . ." His voice trailed off as he thought about an accident he had witnessed as a young man on his neighbor's farm. That one had resulted in a man spending two months in the hospital. Again, Dad silently thanked God for His protection.

The day had started out so well. Jeff had planned

# Jeff McLean: His Courtship

to go through their herd of Polled Hereford cows to decide which he would ship and which he would keep. It was a cool September morning with a light breeze; just the kind of morning that made Jeff even more glad that he had chosen farming as his life's work.

Sarah and Luke had decided to come and spend the weekend at the McLean farm. Jeff and Luke were close friends and enjoyed working together. The plan for this Saturday morning was to get the cattle into a holding pen and then separate those they planned to ship to market. The hay and grain harvest in southern Michigan hadn't been too good this summer, and many farmers were shipping the animals that they wouldn't be able to feed over the winter.

The men had enjoyed their conversation as they worked. They also enjoyed looking over at little one-year-old Judah, who was playing near his mother, Sarah. Judah had just learned to wave, and frequently tried out the new skill on his daddy and his Uncle Jeff.

*Could that have just been this morning?* Jeff asked himself, thinking about how quickly things had changed. Now it looked like the rest of the cattle sorting would have to be done by others while Jeff recovered from his sprain.

Of course, Jeff was something of a hero and all of his younger brothers and sisters crowded around him, asking again and again how it had happened. Nineteen-year-old Janet asked if he had been afraid. Ben, nearly fifteen, and Steve, twelve, hoped that he would have to get a cast, and wondered how long it would be before he could walk again. His youngest sisters, who were nine and seven, asked the most helpful questions. Frequently either Rachel or Becky

# Jeff McLean: His Courtship

would ask, "Can I get you a drink of water, Jeff?" Three-year-old Samuel just seemed to want to bump into the sore leg. At least that's what he kept doing, accidently of course.

"Lunch is about ready," Mom announced. "Jeff, do you think you can come to the table, or do you want me to bring it out here in the living room for you?" she asked kindly.

"I think I can make it," Jeff answered. "The pain is starting to come down a little bit. I'm not very hungry, though. I think I'll at least sit at the table so I can be with everyone."

After the blessing, the talk once again centered on the exciting happenings of the morning. Several new theories were offered as to how the bull got out of his pen. Also, a variety of reasons were suggested as to why the bull would be so angry. "That's just the way bulls are," Dad concluded. "Now you see why I tell you children never to get near them."

"Mom, do you think I can read it now?" Janet asked, looking at her mother.

"Oh, yes, I forgot you got a letter today," Mom said. "Actually, it would be nice to think of something other than angry bulls right now. Why don't you read it?"

"Who's it from?" asked Rachel. "Lydia Prevost or Cindy Hanson?"

"Neither," Janet answered. "It's from a brand new pen-pal that I met through the magazine *Young Women Stepping Heavenward*. Her name is Lisa Harris and she lives only about three hours from us, up in the peninsula." Unfolding the letter, she asked, "Is everyone ready?" When she was sure that she had

13

# Jeff McLean:  His Courtship

everyone's rapt attention (which means she had to pass the ketchup to Becky and the beans were passed to Ben), she began:

Dear Janet,

I'm glad you have decided to be my pen-pal.  As I said in my letter to *Young Women Stepping Heavenward,* I long to be able to write to someone who holds my values and convictions.  It seems like there is no one up here who does, or at least I haven't been able to find them yet.  One thing you can pray for is that I would be able to find like-minded friends.

Well, I will tell you a little about myself.  I just turned twenty years old last month.  In your letter, you told me about your life on a farm.  Well, I live a very different lifestyle.  We live in town and only have a twenty foot by forty foot front yard.  Dad says that is great with him, since he doesn't have to cut so much grass in the summer.  We do have animals, though.  I own tropical fish and the family has a house cat.  Her name is Priscilla and she has long white fur  . . .

Oh, I see I've forgotten to tell you about my family!  Sorry.  My Dad's name is Gerald and he is 47.  He is a manager at the electric company here in town, and everyone thinks he is a wonderful guy (including me ☺).  Mom (Joan) is 43 and so sweet to me.  I have one brother, Caleb, who is 23 and is married to Christine.  My sister, Nancy, is 16.  She is about my size and always likes to borrow my clothes.  Did that ever happen to you when Sarah lived at home? . . .

# Jeff McLean:  His Courtship

In answer to your question, yes, I am committed to courtship.  My brother followed a Biblically-based courtship in marrying Christine.  She is just as sweet as she can be.  My parents are very supportive and want to find God's mate for my life.  We pray about it every night . . .  You said that Sarah followed courtship. Write back and tell me all about how her courtship worked.  There aren't many around here who want to do it, so I am very hungry to learn about the experiences of others.

I suppose I better stop now.  I promised Mom I would bake the bread for supper.  Please write back and tell me more about your family, your farm, and something about your hopes and dreams.  Also, pray that God would make me mature into the Christian woman He wants me to be.

In Christ, Lisa

P.S.  Can you send a picture of yourself?  It's not important if you can't, but I do like to have a picture of my pen pals.

As soon as Janet finished reading, Ben commented, "Dad, imagine only having to cut a yard as small as they have.  That sure would be easy."

Dad smiled at the family's principal grass cutter. "Yes, Ben, it would be easier.  But don't you think it would also be sort of small to do things in?"  Ben smiled and nodded.

Janet looked at Sarah.  "Do you mind me telling Lisa about your courtship experiences?"

# Jeff McLean: His Courtship

Sarah smiled and gave Luke's hand a squeeze. "Not at all! I'm so thankful for my courtship experience. Luke is the husband that God had planned for me. I'm not sure I would have married the right man if Mom and Dad hadn't been involved in our courtship."

"But don't you miss living on a farm?" Becky asked. "You used to say how much you liked living on the farm here."

Sarah didn't hesitate to answer. "I do like living on a farm, Becky. But I most like living wherever my husband decides for us to live. I married a carpenter, not a farmer. I'm happy to live right where I do."

The talk eventually turned back to the cattle and how the rest of the day should be spent. It was decided that Jeff should take it easy and that Dad and Luke would finish sorting the cattle. Of course Jeff would be on the sidelines as much as possible, giving his opinion as to which should be shipped.

All too soon, the sun began to set in the western sky. The cattle were sorted and ready for shipping on Monday morning. Jeff's ankle started to swell which resulted in orders from Mom to sit down and stay down! Everyone settled down on the back porch to watch the colors change in the autumn sky. As they sat there talking, Jeff thought to himself about the changes in his herd. On Monday, twenty head would be shipped. He had seen all of those animals right after they were born, had nursed some to health, and had made sure they had many gallons of water over the years as well as thousands of bales of hay. Now they were going. Changes. Life was about changes and how you dealt with them. With God's help no change was impossible to handle, of that he was sure.

What changes would occur in his own life over the next weeks, months, and years? Where was he headed? While he was sure he wanted to be a farmer, many other questions remained. Where would he find a farm that he could afford? How would he get set up on his farm? What kinds of animals and crops should he raise? And was he to live on the farm alone, or was God going to bring a wife into his life? As he had on many occasions, once again Jeff committed all of these questions into God's hands. God would reveal His will in His timing. The sky changed from a bright pink to a soft violet. *What changes are ahead for me?* he wondered.

# Chapter Two

Monday began as a cloudy, windy day with a threat of thunderstorms building in the western sky.  It was only eight o'clock and yet the McLean household was already humming with activity.  A casual passerby would have been surprised to learn that just yesterday the family had observed a quiet, restful Sunday.  Now, everything and everybody seemed to be moving at a terrific pace.

After making breakfast with Janet's help, Mom had moved to the sewing machine.  She was working hard to finish several winter jumpers for the younger girls.  Of course, she also spent a good deal of her time settling disputes, providing guidance and instruction when needed, and planning the meals.

Ben and Steve were out doing chores in the barn.  There were three large stock tanks to fill with water and fresh bedding to be added in the cows' loafing shed. The chickens had to be fed and watered, and any new eggs picked up.  It wasn't as important to gather the eggs quickly as it had been in the heat of the summer.  Still, Mom liked those fresh eggs to move from the barn to her refrigerator as soon as possible.

Janet was just finishing milking the family's four milk goats.  Their milk production was down from their summer high.  In July and August, when the goats were getting the most fresh pasture, they had provided over four gallons of milk a day.  That was too much even for a family the size of the McLeans, and Janet had enjoyed finding several families in the

18

community who appreciated the value of wholesome milk. One family had a son with leukemia, so they were especially thankful for the opportunity to buy a product that might help build up his immune system.

Rachel and Becky were busy cleaning the kitchen and doing the breakfast dishes. When they were finished with that, they would begin working on the laundry. "I love to do the laundry," Becky often related to a guest in her cheerful way. "It's so much fun to see the clothes go from dirty to clean in just one day!" The girls also helped with some of the light cooking and helped clean the house.

Even little Samuel was busy. Although he was only three years old, he was able to put away the silverware after Rachel and Becky had dried them. He was also responsible for helping Steve empty the garbage in the house. Mom and Dad felt it was very important that everyone in the house do some chores in order to learn responsibility and contribute in a meaningful way to the welfare of the home.

Although Jeff's ankle had healed a lot and the swelling was almost gone, it had turned several shades of black and dark blue. He still favored that leg and tried not to put much weight on it. Yet, he was moving among the cattle in the pens and checking on the herd in the pasture trying to act as though this were any other Monday. "Dad, wasn't Shorty supposed to be here before 8:00 this morning?" Shorty was an elderly neighbor-friend who often transported the McLeans' cattle to market. He insisted that everyone old and young call him Shorty.

Dad finished tightening a bolt on the corral fence before talking. "There, that should hold Giant in," he

# Jeff McLean: His Courtship

said.  Turning to Jeff, he added, "Yes, Shorty said he
wanted to get our animals early this morning because
he had two more places to stop and pick up animals.
The auction starts at 11:00."  Looking at the darken-
ing sky, he commented,  "I sure hope he hasn't run
into any trouble."

"I think I'll call and see if he's left yet," Jeff
volunteered.  "Maybe he's having trouble getting the
stock truck going again."

"Good idea," Dad agreed.  "I would like to get
these loaded before that storm hits.  Thunder, light-
ning, and loading cattle just don't mix."

In a few minutes, Jeff returned.  "Mabel said that
Shorty left about five minutes ago.  Guess he did have
some trouble this morning getting that old truck
going."

Dad smiled.  "Old trucks and old tractors and old
machinery.  That seems to be the lot of us all, doesn't
it?"

"It sure does," Jeff agreed.  One of the McLean
tractors had failed to start this morning and was right
now getting its battery charged.  "But that's okay," he
reflected.  "At least we don't owe the bank a ton of
money on the equipment we do have.  I'd hate to be
like some of those guys about our size who are in a lot
of debt for brand new tractors and equipment."

Dad didn't say anything.  Yet, he was pleased that
his son had caught his own value for being as debt-free
as possible.  Most young men were willing to go in
debt just as far as the lenders would allow them.  Such
behavior was totally unwise in Dad's eyes.

Before long, both men turned their heads as they
heard an old truck rumbling toward their farm.

# Jeff McLean: His Courtship

"There's Shorty now!" Jeff said, even before the truck came in view. "Couldn't mistake his old truck for any other."

Sure enough, Shorty pulled in and backed up to the corral fence. Ben and Steve appeared, seemingly out of nowhere, to watch the action.

"Sorry I'm running late, boys." Shorty took out a handkerchief and blew his nose. "Had a little trouble convincing the old truck to get going this morning. Got them ready to go?" he asked, motioning his hand toward the cattle in the corral.

"Yes, I think so," Dad said. "We have twenty to ship today. Jeff and I have been trying to decide how many to ship. It's hard to know. The hay sure hasn't been good this year, though." It was obvious that Dad didn't really want to have to ship all of these cattle. Sure, he always shipped some at this time of year. But he was having to part with some of his young heifers and steers. Oh well, it couldn't be helped.

"You're not alone, David," Shorty said. "I've been hauling cattle and pigs for most of your neighbors the last several weeks. Nope, you're not alone."

"Dad, can I help load them?" Steve asked.

"I think not this time," Dad replied. "Some of these are bound to be a little balky at walking up that ramp and I would prefer to know that you are safe right where you are."

Steve dropped his head in disappointment, but didn't say anything. *When will I be old enough?* he wondered.

Dad noticed Steve's disappointment. "Getting to rake hay for the first time this summer was pretty exciting, wasn't it? Did you tell Shorty about that?"

# Jeff McLean: His Courtship

Steve quickly forgot his sadness and filled Shorty in on the details.

"Well, I'd say you're sure growing up," Shorty said. Then turning to Jeff he added, "I remember when you were telling me about the same thing as Steve just told me. Yet, now you're grown. How old are you, Jeff?"

"Twenty-two," Jeff replied.

"Yep, I thought so," Shorty nodded with a grin. "Why, I remember" . . . but then stopped when a peal of thunder sounded in the distance. "We better get these cattle loaded up so someone else can play with them this winter."

Ben smiled at that. Imagine someone actually playing with a 1500 pound animal!

Most of the animals loaded pretty well. But old "125" had no intention of walking up that plank and getting into that trailer. She spread her back legs and braced her front ones, trying to act as much like a mule as she could. Jeff tried coaxing her with grain. Dad tried talking to her. But she wouldn't budge. Shorty finally tied some rope to the trailer, looped it behind her, and the three men began pulling on the other end of the rope. Slowly but surely she walked forward into the trailer.

The only other troublemaker was one of the two young bulls. He started up the ramp and it looked like he was going to be no problem. Then, unexpectedly he turned and started back down the ramp. That caused one of the steers to back up suddenly, pinning Dad against the corral fence. He wasn't really hurt, but got his arm and left side bruised in the process. Steve was better able to see the wisdom in his dad's refusal to let him help today.

"Jeff, if you're not busy, Mrs. Walters is on the phone and would like to talk to you," Janet called from the kitchen door.

"Go ahead, son. We've got this under control now," Dad reassured him.

"Okay, but I'll be right back," Jeff said. "I wonder if her roof is leaking again?" Mrs. Walters was a widow who owned a run-down farm about a mile down the road. Her husband had died when Jeff was fifteen, and he had taken her on as his personal project. Mrs. Walters had gratefully accepted his assistance down through the years, and had come to depend on him.

"Thanks, Janet," Jeff smiled, taking the phone from her as he entered the house. "Hello, this is Jeff," he said into the receiver. "How are you, Mrs. Walters? That roof isn't leaking again is it?"

Mrs. Walters laughed. "No, the roof seems to be fine. It hasn't leaked in . . . Get down, Tabby!" Jeff heard the phone fall to the floor, and a cat's long meow. "Sorry, but that silly cat won't leave me alone when I'm on the phone," Mrs. Walters said, resuming her conversation. "I think she wishes she could talk, too." There was a long pause as she tried to remember why she had called. "Jeff, can you come by sometime this week?"

"I'll be glad to," Jeff replied. "What kind of tools should I bring along? Plumbing, electrical, or what?"

"Oh, just bring yourself," she replied. "All I need is you. Think you can come before Wednesday?"

"Yes, I'll try. I'll see if I can run over there later this morning. Actually, I'll have to drive since my leg isn't doing great."

"Good!" Mrs. Walters praised.  "But what happened to your leg?"

"I can tell you when I see you," Jeff said, looking out the window at his father and Shorty, who were having trouble getting the ramp to slide back into its holder under the truck.  "It's nothing really.  I'll see you soon."

And soon it was.  Within fifteen minutes, Shorty was pulling out of the McLeans' driveway, the truck sounding like it had a lot more weight on it than when it pulled in just an hour earlier.  After making sure the fences were all securely fastened, Jeff told his dad about the phone call.  Ten minutes later, Jeff was standing at Mrs. Walters' door.

"Come in! Come in!" she invited.  As Jeff walked through the tiny entry toward the living room, he couldn't help noticing the condition of the house. Even though he had spent a good bit of time helping her keep the place going, Mrs. Walters' house was not in good shape.  Several windows had cracks, the linoleum was peeling in the kitchen, and the whole house needed painting inside and out. Of course, that was nothing compared to the major things that needed fixing.  It desperately needed a new roof, the electrical service was outdated and somewhat dangerous, the well was just about to need replacing, and the basement walls had begun to crack.  When one left the house and examined the outbuildings on the farm, things didn't look brighter.  The barn needed some new siding, and it needed painting and electrical work. The chicken house and old milk house were pretty much dilapidated.  About all they could use was a

# Jeff McLean: His Courtship

good wrecking ball. The fencing and cross fencing hadn't been maintained or repaired in over ten years. Mr. Walters' health hadn't allowed him to have animals for the last five years of his life. The pastures and hay fields were overgrown also.

As Jeff thought about all of the problems with Mrs. Walters' farm, he was made even more thankful for his parents' farm. There simply was no comparison between the two.

"Have a seat," Mrs. Walters suggested. Jeff was reluctant, since he had his "barn clothes" on. "No, don't worry about your clothes. Have a seat!" she insisted. Jeff obeyed.

"My, you're growing up," she said, looking Jeff over.

*That's two people today who have commented about my age*, thought Jeff. *Am I aging quickly or something?*

"Jeff, you've mentioned to me several times that you thought you were going to be a farmer. Is that still true?"

Jeff looked at the manure on his pants' leg and smiled. "Yes ma'am. I guess you could say I'm already a farmer!" he laughed.

Mrs. Walters laughed also. "Yes, I know you are working with your dad. But are you planning on owning your own farm some day?"

Jeff was a little uneasy. Sure, he had thought about that. A lot. He wasn't sure how it was all going to work out, though. Dad was still a young man with a growing family to support, and needed all of his farm to supply the needed income. Although he and Dad had talked about it some, nothing specific had ever been decided. They had looked at a few farms, but all had been too expensive.

"Yes, I do want to own a farm some day. But I guess that won't happen for a while," Jeff finally answered.

"Let's make it happen sooner, rather than later," Mrs. Walters said. With that, she took a deep breath, folded her arms, sat back in her chair, and looked at Jeff with a serious, yet satisfied, expression on her face.

Jeff didn't know what to say or do. When Mrs. Walters continued to stare at him, he finally managed to mumble something like "I suppose so."

Mrs. Walters realized that Jeff didn't have a clue as to what she was talking about. "I'm going to sell my farm. And I want you to buy it!" she announced.

Now Jeff really didn't know what to say. He had never thought about buying her farm. In fact, he never really thought of it as a farm. It was more just a house that needed constant repair and his attention.

"That's nice . . . I mean, thank you," he said, haltingly. Jeff turned his head to look out of the window at the barn.

"Well, I can see I've surprised you." She looked around the room. "I know it's not as nice as it once was, Jeff, but it could be fixed up. My son-in-law has finally convinced me to move to Florida near them. Imagine never having to worry about snow again! Anyway, you think about my farm and we'll talk more later. Okay?"

"Yes, ma'am," Jeff agreed.

His mind was whirling as he left Mrs. Walters' house. *Would I like to own her farm?* he thought. It

# Jeff McLean: His Courtship

sure had a lot of acreage with it, something that was hard to come by today. And the soil was good. But oh, the buildings were in such a bad state! It would take a lot of work to get them in good shape. A lot of work! *And when am I going to find time to work on it?* Dad needed his help on the family farm.

Then it dawned on him that he had no idea how much she was asking for the farm. Although he had saved some money, he doubted that he could afford even such a run-down place as hers. *How much will it cost?* he thought.

His mind continued to race as he slowly drove home. The day had cleared off after all and the sun was shining brightly. Pulling into his parents' driveway, he saw Mom carrying some laundry out to the clothesline. Everything on the farm looked so clean and fixed up. *It would certainly be easier just to live here at home*, he thought.

As he parked the pickup truck, he saw his dad emerge from behind some sheets blowing in the breeze. Dad was helping Mom pin up some wash cloths while he talked to her. That started Jeff thinking in a new vein. If he did buy Mrs. Walters' farm, would there be someone to share his life with? So many questions, yet so few answers. *Dear God, help me to know Your will for my life*, he prayed.

# Chapter Three

Well, son, I guess our cows are being sold about now," Dad said at lunch. "The prices for live beef were down a little bit last Friday. I wonder what they'll go for today?"

Jeff passed some black-eyed peas and answered, "I wonder, too. Tony Barrett was telling me last week that he thought the price would continue to come down. Seems that a lot of Texas ranches are selling off cattle, too, because of the drought they've had down there. It's been a rough weather year for lots of us." He thought a minute and added, "Did Shorty say he was going to call with the prices?"

"No," Dad replied. "I suppose we'll hear tomorrow how we did. Kate, could you get me some more water, please? " Dad asked. Then looking at Jeff, he asked, "Was it Mrs. Walters' roof that needed attention this time? She really is going to have to break down and replace those shingles soon."

"Her roof is fine," Jeff responded. *Should I bring it up now? Why not?* he thought. "Dad, has Mrs. Walters talked to you about anything . . . you know . . . anything important recently?"

"Like what?" Dad asked, a look of slight concern on his face.

"About her selling her farm."

"Well, she's finally going to sell, is she? I've been expecting that announcement for several years. There's no way she can keep up that big farm by herself." Then remembering the question that Jeff actually asked, he answered, "And no, she didn't tell me anything about selling it. Has she chosen a real estate company yet?"

"I don't think so," Jeff answered. "In fact, I don't think she intends to list the farm with an agent. She," he hesitated, then continued, ". . . she hopes to sell it to me."

Dad was obviously surprised. In fact, everyone, even Samuel, got quiet quickly. Samuel turned to Becky and stated, importantly, "Jeff's going to buy Mrs. Walters' farm, Becky!"

"No he's not," she replied. "Or is he, Dad?"

Dad seemed in a serious mood all of a sudden. "I don't know. I suppose you'll have to ask Jeff that question."

All eyes were on Jeff. Now he wished that he hadn't brought it up at the lunch table. It would have been much better to seek his dad in private and talk to him about it.

"I don't know!" was the reply that Jeff finally gave to Becky's continual stare. "There's more that I don't know about it than I do know. Dad, can we just talk about this more later?"

"Sure, son," Dad answered, noticing Jeff's uneasiness. He changed the subject to help matters. "Has anyone heard the weather forecast today?"

Mom said she thought it was supposed to stay sunny, at least that was her hope when she hung out her clothes. Steve said he had seen clouds in the north. Before long, the conversation was shifted to the chores for the afternoon and the homeschooling lessons that still needed work.

# Jeff McLean: His Courtship

It seemed odd to Jeff that Dad didn't bring up the topic of Mrs. Walters' farm that afternoon as the two of them worked together. Right before supper, Jeff felt like talking about it and asked, "Dad, isn't it strange that Mrs. Walters didn't talk to you about her farm?"

Dad got that serious look on his face again. "I would think that she might mention it to me," he replied. "You remember that I asked her a few years ago if we could come in and rework her hay fields. For some strange reason she really didn't want to." He tightened the fence he was working on a little more, then added, "I suppose that she didn't talk to me first, because she wants to sell it to you. And because," he added with emphasis, "she must consider you to be a man."

Jeff hadn't thought of that. *She considers me a man?* The more he thought about that, the more he liked it. Well, he certainly wasn't a boy anymore.

Dad noticed Jeff's countenance and smiled. "Just remember that I'm always here for you if you need any help or counsel."

"I know that," Jeff returned quickly. "I wouldn't think of making any kind of move without talking to you. The fact is that I don't know much about the situation. I don't even know how much she's going to ask for her farm."

"That would be one of the earlier things you should find out," Dad replied. He stretched another section of fence. "In fact there are many things you'll want to learn. I'm sure you've probably already started thinking about them."

Jeff was thankful for his father. Here was a man

who would help him  think of the right questions to ask.  "I'm not sure I know where to begin," Jeff admitted.

The two men talked a lot about the kinds of information that Jeff needed in order to make a wise decision.  Before they had finished, Dad noticed that it was time to head to the house for supper.  "I think we had better start moving toward the house," Dad suggested.  "Mom's fish should be coming out of the oven any minute now.  We've got plenty of time to talk more about this important matter.  What do you say?"

"I'd say that, at least right now, I would much prefer Mom's fish to any farm for sale in the state! Let's go."

Over the next several weeks, Jeff and Dad were able to work through many of the issues that sur- rounded Mrs. Walters' farm.  They learned the price and were amazed at how low it was.  "Did she tell you how she came up with the price?" Dad asked, aston- ished at the figure reported by Jeff.

"I asked her if she didn't think that maybe she was selling it too low.  I don't want to cheat her, Dad," Jeff replied.

"I know," Dad said quickly.  "I was just curious."

Jeff seemed a little reluctant to speak.  "She said that I had done so much work for her over the years, and had been so kind, that she just wanted me to get the farm.  I quickly told her that I hadn't been helping her in order to get something in return.  All she said was, 'I know!  That's why I want you to have it so badly!'  The more I talked about the price, the more set she seemed to be about it."

# Jeff McLean: His Courtship

"Even so, you don't have that much money set aside," Dad said. "I wish there was some way I could . . ."

Before Dad could finish, Jeff jumped in. "I know you would like to help financially, Dad. But you've still got a lot of mouths to feed and worry about here on the farm. Even though I don't have enough money, she wants me to pay the balance on a five-year land contract, which simply means I will pay payments to her for the balance over the next five years. Of course, she would still hold the title to the land until I had paid all of the money. She insists that she won't accept any interest, either!" Jeff paused. "I need to pray more about the land contract. I don't really want to be in debt, but how else can a young man get started and buy a farm? I'm going to study God's Word some more and see if I get a peace about it."

"That's wise," Dad responded. "Of course, even with the purchase price resolved, you still have to think about all of the repair and maintenance to the place. That all costs money."

"What do you suggest I do about that, Dad? I mean, I'm not even sure how much it would cost me to make the repairs, even if I supply all the labor myself."

"You can do what I would do in a case like that," Dad responded. "I would seek the counsel of godly men and see what they say." He thought for a minute. "I would recommend that you ask Bud Nelson to walk the property with you. He's a Christian carpenter and builder and can probably not only give you a rough estimate of what the materials might cost, but can also probably give you some pointers about how to save money and time.  Maybe Luke can also give you some ideas when he comes to visit us again.  He's quite a carpenter, too!"

"That's a great idea," Jeff replied enthusiastically. "And maybe you could give me your thoughts about getting the pastures and hay fields back in good shape?"

"I would be glad to," Dad assured him.  "Why don't we plan on spending tomorrow morning looking it over more closely?  That pasture right next to the road is still in pretty good shape . . ."

And so the men talked and planned, and Jeff dreamed.

A few evenings later,  Mr. Nelson pulled in the driveway.  "Hi, Bud!" Dad said.  "I suppose you're here to go with Jeff to look at the farm.  Can you come in for a while?"

"Hello, David," Bud replied.  "Thanks, but we need to get to the farm.  My wife has asked me to try and be home by 8:30 so I can help her move some furniture.  Seems late in the year for spring cleaning, but you know Jane!  Last night, a spool of thread rolled behind the couch and when she went to retrieve it, she was horrified at the amount of dust she found back there.  So, I'm going to help her move some furniture so she can do what she enjoys doing.  Cleaning!"

"You certainly have one of the cleanest homes around, Bud.  We should be thankful for wives who want to keep things looking good.  They don't all care, you know."

"That's true!" Bud replied.  "Ready, Jeff?  You coming too, David?"

# Jeff McLean: His Courtship

Soon the three men were poring over the buildings. Jeff had brought along a notebook to record Mr. Nelson's comments. There was certainly a lot to write down. Yet, somehow hearing Mr. Nelson talk about the repairs, it didn't seem so overwhelming. "You'll just have to take your time, Jeff, and not feel like you have to get it all done in a month or so," Mr. Nelson instructed. "Just break it all down into specific tasks, prioritize them, and start working. Your biggest enemy in the project will be yourself. If you're not careful, you'll expect too much progress too soon. Just slow down, and work your plan. It can all be done and you can do almost all of it yourself!

"What an interesting old barn!" Bud Nelson exclaimed, as he opened a side door. "Would be hard to build one of these today!" As they ventured into the hayloft, Mr. Nelson pointed out several rafters which would need to be strengthened.

As he moved to look more closely at one rafter, Jeff suddenly felt the floor give way. He reached out and tried to grab hold of something, but nothing seemed solid. He felt himself falling though the hayloft floor and onto the lower level. He was thankful that there were two or three musty, rotten bales of hay to break his fall or he probably would have hurt himself pretty badly.

Jeff looked up into the concerned faces of the men in the hayloft. Looking beyond the men, he could see the inside of the barn's roof. There was daylight streaming through several holes and cracks there. *What am I getting myself into?* he thought, as he tried to brush some of the rotten hay out of his hair. More hay had fallen down the back of his shirt. *What am I getting myself into?* Just minutes before he was feeling more confident that this would be a good farm to buy. Now he was a little depressed about the prospects.

Dad and Bud were glad that Jeff wasn't hurt physically, but both could easily see the less-than-enthusiastic expression on his face. Bud spoke up. "I'll tell you what, Jeff. I know this place isn't perfect. But do you know what a perfect farm would cost you? How soon do you think you could afford a farm that had no bad wiring, no leaky roof, no . . . no rotten hay in the barn?" At that moment Jeff sneezed, and all three men broke out in laughter.

"I wouldn't blame you for not being excited about the place," Dad consoled Jeff. "But I think what I hear Bud saying is that everything, with the exception of two outbuildings, is structurally sound. It just needs a lot of sweat to be poured into it. What you have to decide is whether you want to invest that sweat."

Jeff got up and dusted himself off as well as he could. "You know I'm not afraid of hard work. I just want to make a wise decision."

"Keep praying about the matter," Bud suggested. "I believe God will give you wisdom." With that the three men headed back to Dad's farm.

Over the next several days, Jeff continued to explore the farm. Mrs. Walters was always kind and didn't seem in a hurry for Jeff to decide. In fact, she seemed pleased that he would take the matter so seriously. "You're going to be a good husband and father someday," she beamed. "Don't jump into things and you'll save yourself a lot of grief. That's what my

# Jeff McLean: His Courtship

husband always said."

The weather was definitely turning cooler. It took longer for it to warm up in the mornings and it cooled off faster in the evenings.

Work around the farm continued, but at a much slower pace. More family time was spent homeschooling when the weather turned cooler. Jeff and Janet both helped Mom do some of the schooling. Janet, especially, had always been good at math and could explain it easily. Family members had more time to write letters to their friends. There was also a slower pace at meal times. No longer was it necessary to eat quickly and get out to the hayfields, for which everyone was grateful.

"I know how God created things," Samuel said at breakfast one morning.

Mom smiled. "Yes, we read the story about creation yesterday, didn't we, Samuel? Do you want to tell Daddy about it?"

Samuel felt important. He scooped up some eggs and began to talk with his mouth full. Mom corrected him for this. So, when he had finished swallowing, he began. "God said, 'Let there be trees.' And trees popped up! And He said, 'Let there be flowers.' And flowers popped up! And He said, 'Let there be people and they popped up!" Samuel didn't notice that Becky and Rachel were doing everything they could not to laugh out loud. Samuel took a big drink of milk, then got a serious look on his face. "Then God said, 'Let there be houses . . .'" Samuel's eyes got very big, ". . . and the people built the houses!"

"Are you sure those houses didn't just pop up?" queried Ben, suppressing a laugh.

# Jeff McLean:  His Courtship

"No," Samuel repeated, knowingly. "The people built them." Looking at Dad, he asked, "Didn't they, Dad?"

"Yes, Samuel," Dad reassured his son. "The people built the houses. Of course, God gave them strength and wisdom to know how to build them."

"Uh huh," Samuel said, looking over at his brothers and sisters with a smile of satisfaction. That was one Bible story he felt sure he had mastered.

Even though things on the farm were slowing down, Jeff realized that he had to give Mrs. Walters a decision soon. As he sat in his room on a Sunday evening, he turned the issues over in his mind. He had told Mrs. Walters that he would give her an answer by tomorrow morning.

It looked like there was going to be a lot of work to do. Yet, he could do much of it during the colder months when things slowed down on the farm. Summer was too busy, but the rest of the year he had a good bit of time he could devote to Mrs. Walters' farm. Also, he was amazed at the number of men who had volunteered to help him do some of the work. Apparently, word had gotten out into the community that Jeff was considering making this move and many men wanted to see him get set up on his own place.

The cost of materials for the repairs could certainly add up fast. However, several men had suggested that Jeff buy materials from auctions to save money. Mr. Jeffers, who was retired, had even promised to bid on materials in Jeff's absence, knowing that Jeff didn't have much time to go to auctions since most were held in the summer months. Luke had suggested the

# Jeff McLean: His Courtship

possibility of buying an old barn, tearing it down, and using the lumber. Such barns did become available from time to time as farmers attempted to clear old homesteads in order to have more land to till. Of course, tearing down an old barn would also take a great deal of time. Dad had reminded Jeff that he could time his purchases carefully, buying new materials only when they were on sale at local stores and building supply houses.

Although Jeff wasn't excited about having to use a land contract, he realized that was probably the only way he could get started in farming. At least he wouldn't have to take out an expensive bank loan and pay interest and fees. If beef market prices improved, Jeff planned on making even larger payments, and thus own the farm sooner.

One of his biggest hesitations was the amount of sheer effort and time it would take. He was sure there would be many exhausting days over the next several years, but he was young, wasn't he? Better to make a move like this now, while he was young enough to stand up to the sweat and toil.

Finally, Jeff thought about the fact that the purchase of Mrs. Walters' farm would put him on a track that would eventually move him out of his parents' home. He had known that he would eventually move away from home and he wasn't afraid to live alone. Yet, life would be different. He would miss seeing Samuel's sparkling eyes at the breakfast table, and hearing him ask Jeff what he could do to help on the farm today. He would miss family devotions and hearing Becky's sweet, innocent prayers. He would miss the fun and laughter that occurred when Dad

# Jeff McLean: His Courtship

would sometimes start telling stories of his childhood after supper. So many other things would be missed. How had Mr. Slocum put it? "Moving out of your parents' home is one of the happiest times you can imagine. Moving out is one of the saddest times you can imagine. It's a fact!" Well, Jeff was beginning to understand more about what Mr. Slocum must have meant by that. So much would be missed. Yet, what good things might God do through the home of Jeff McLean? He was excited about the possibilities.

Jeff had prayed for God's wisdom in making a decision. He had talked to a number of godly men and asked a number of individuals to pray for him as well. He knew he would have to trust that God would give him peace about the correct decision. In weighing all the factors, it seemed to Jeff that buying Mrs. Walters' farm was God's will for his life. Tomorrow, Jeff would have a talk with her.

As he shut off the light and crawled into bed, Jeff anticipated a rather difficult time going to sleep. After all, this was a very big decision in his life. Surprisingly, he was asleep in a matter of minutes.

# Chapter Four

On Monday morning, Jeff visited Mrs. Walters and agreed to buy her farm. Mrs. Walters was thrilled and said that her lawyer would be contacting Jeff within the week. *Well, I've done it!* Jeff thought. He felt both excited and a little nervous. *I hope I've made the right decision.*

God seemed to impress upon Jeff what a blessing it was to be able to buy a farm at such a reasonable price. Then, as he drove home, it dawned afresh how close his farm would be to his parents' farm. Anytime he wanted to, he could be there in just a few minutes. Why, he could even ride his bike there! *Thank You Lord Jesus, for blessing me so much,* he prayed. *Help me not to complain or doubt your provision for my life.*

As soon as the paperwork was signed, Mrs. Walters made arrangements for moving out of her house. Jeff helped her pack up some of her things and the two had many wonderful talks. They talked about the history of the farm and all the hopes and dreams that Mr. Walters had for the place. Jeff learned some very interesting stories, which he could someday relate to his own children, about how the farm was operated in its very early years. Mrs. Walters also explained how the fields had been drained. She even found a map, drawn by a civil engineer, outlining exactly how to drain a few other places that needed some work. These were to prove very helpful to Jeff in the next several years. In a matter of weeks, Mrs. Walters

# Jeff McLean: His Courtship

drove away, leaving Jeff to begin work on his farm. He had already decided to continue living at home until it was in better shape, especially since he was still very actively involved in his dad's farm.

As fall turned to winter, Jeff took pleasure in driving to his new farm and working on it. Of course, some of the work was very hard. The bitter cold weather didn't help matters either. Still, he tried to keep a positive attitude with the help of God. After all, he was fixing up his own farm! He was also encouraged when help was provided by family and friends.

One chilly winter night brought over two feet of wet snow to lower Michigan, with drifts as high as six feet in some places. It was certainly beautiful, yet many were worried about the heavy loads on their roofs. Jeff was no exception. After working at home, shoveling many cubic feet of snow from paths and roofs, he ventured to his own farmstead. Using the ladder that Mrs. Walters had left, he climbed to the top of his house. It was an old-fashioned house with lots of dormers, so the roof had many valleys and different pitches. "Just the kind of roof that would like to cave in on me," he said out loud as he began to shovel. "Even if it doesn't cave in, I suspect all of this snow could cause ice buildup and more water leaks in the house. Well, we'll see what I can do to prevent that."

The more snow that Jeff shoveled off the house, the more there seemed to be. In some of the valleys of the roof the snow came up to his chest. Still, he didn't quit. After cleaning the west side of the roof, he crawled over the top to the other side and began to work on it. Maybe it was because he was tired.

# Jeff McLean:  His Courtship

Maybe it was because he didn't really know how close he was.  For whatever reason, Jeff got too close to the edge of the roof.  It was slippery there, due to snow that had fallen earlier in the week and melted, and then frozen again.  Before he knew what was happening, Jeff slipped off the roof and fell a story and a half to the ground below.

He hit hard, with a thump and a crack so loud he was sure he would keep hearing it for a few days.  Thankfully, the large amount of snow broke his fall somewhat.  It was something like falling into a large pillow.  On the other hand, it was like falling onto a pillow that was resting on a concrete floor.  Deep, heavy wet snow covered the lower half of Jeff's body, trapping him under its weight.  When he tried to move to pick himself up, he found that one arm wasn't working correctly and it hurt terribly anytime he moved it.  *It can't be broken,* he thought.  *I forgot to tell Mom and Dad that was I coming here.  It may take a while before someone comes and helps me.*

Soon, he forgot about the pain in his arm as a wave of nausea overcame him.  He starting going into shock and realized that his vision wasn't working properly.  There were tiny specks of black everywhere and he couldn't seem to get rid of them.  Then the pain in his arm got worse.  Jeff slumped into unconsciousness.

When he came to, it was getting dark.  Jeff tried again to climb out of the deep snow, but the effort was too much for him.  If he could only use both arms!  But as the left one was limp and dangling that was out of the question.  He was cold.  Very cold.  Snow had fallen into his clothes when he hit the ground and it had melted from his body heat so that his clothes were wet. His face and hands were numb. *Frostbite*, he thought. *I've got to keep from getting frostbite*. Jeff attempted to rub his face and hands but his arm hurt so badly that he had to quit. Those specks of black returned and he was close to becoming unconscious again. *Dear Heavenly Father, please help me not to pass out*, Jeff prayed earnestly. *Please help me to stay awake. And please help someone to find me. I ask these things, knowing that You can do anything. Yet, I ask Your will to be done. Please help me, Father.*

Jeff heard the sound of a car. Was it his parents coming to check on him? Surely, he must have been laying here at least three hours. The sound of the car faded away and so did some of his hope. Again, he prayed that God would strengthen him.

It got darker. The sky was leaden gray, with the threat of another snow storm brewing. Jeff fought sleep, yet it seemed the only way to peace. His body no longer felt the cold. If someone didn't come soon, Jeff knew that he would suffer long-term effects from the exposure.

The sound of another car. More hope that this nightmare would end. Yes, it seemed to Jeff that the car had pulled into his farm's driveway. He heard voices. Finally, he heard Janet scream. "Dad, he's back here!" Soon Dad and Janet were ministering to Jeff's needs. They dug him out of the snow, and laid their coats on him to get him warm. Dad ran to the car and came back with some rags that he used to fashion a crude sling for Jeff's arm.

"Can you stand up and walk, Jeff?" Dad asked.

"I can't, Dad," Jeff answered weakly.

# Jeff McLean: His Courtship

"It's all right, son. We'll get you out," Dad reassured. Dad took off Jeff's gloves and looked at his hands. Sighing, he spoke, "Jeff, it would help if you could put your hands under your arms to warm them up slowly. Can you do that?"

"My arm hurts too badly, Dad," Jeff said weakly. "I can try rubbing them together."

"No, that wouldn't be good," Dad replied. "Don't worry, we'll get you out of this cold weather now."

Dad quickly scanned the area, looking for something. Not finding anything useful nearby, he commented, "I guess we'll have to take our coats back and make a stretcher from them, son." Dad tied the arms of his and Janet's coats together and then carefully slid the coats under Jeff. "Janet, you hold this edge up and walk along behind me. Keep Jeff's arm and neck slightly off the snow so he doesn't bump anything. Can you do that?"

"I think so," Janet answered.

Using the other edge of the makeshift stretcher, Dad half-skidded, half-dragged Jeff toward the car. The two struggled to make progress. It wasn't easy with all the snow and Jeff's weight, but slowly, they inched forward.

In about ten minutes, Dad and Janet had reached the car and tugged Jeff into the back seat, trying hard not to jostle the injured limb more than necessary.

Although the warmth of Dad's car felt good at first, after a while it made his face and hands start to hurt again. And the nausea was back. Dad rushed Jeff to the emergency room, where it was learned that he had broken his arm in two places. He also had some frostbite. "He might have some trouble with the cold

# Jeff McLean: His Courtship

weather bothering him from now on," the doctor had said. "We'll just have to wait and see."

The next several weeks were times of recovery and healing. In another month, Jeff was at the farm, doing some simple tasks, and helping direct the many volunteers who came to help him.

Before long, he seemed his old self again. However, the cold did seem colder to him than it had in the past. Maybe the frostbite would have some negative long-term effects after all.

As he worked at his farm, he realized that something was missing. Sure, he had hay fields and pasture, a barn and some outbuildings, and a house. What was missing? A family to live there and enjoy and work on the farm. It seemed to Jeff that God, during those months, was revealing that he was to start searching for God's mate for his life. Jeff made it a matter of prayer.

In early February, Jeff was helping his dad get hay for the cows one morning. He felt like he couldn't wait any longer to talk about his future. "Dad," he started confidingly, "I feel that God has been speaking to me lately about something very important and I wanted to talk to you about it."

Dad stopped throwing hay bales, and put his hands in his pockets to try and warm them up. It was a very cold morning, and even though he had been wearing gloves, his hands still felt like ice cubes. "I'm always here, Jeff."

"Dad, I think I'm ready to start finding God's mate for my life." He paused. He seemed at a loss for words. *What more is there to say?* he wondered.

He didn't have to say anything else because Dad

quickly jumped in. "I'm sure you've prayed about this. Let's go in and get warmed up and talk by the fire. Okay?"

In a few minutes, the men were sitting in the kitchen next to the wood burning stove, drinking hot chocolate. "You know, Jeff, I feel that a man is ready to begin the process of courtship when he has matured as a Christian and is ready to take on the responsibilities of leading his home. I've thought about this a lot. How can we know if we have the right characteristics? Which things would be most important?"

Dad waited for Jeff to answer. "I suppose we should search the Scripture to see what God's measure of a godly man really is," Jeff offered. "There are lots of passages that tell us how men, and husbands specifically, are supposed to live their lives. That would be a good place to begin."

"Excellent!" Dad responded. "There's nothing more important for us to be doing. Let's look at a few right now." Turning in his Bible, Dad read several passages from Titus 1, I Peter 5, and I Timothy 3. "These speak specifically about what to look for in an elder or deacon. Now I know you're not an elder, and don't feel you're ready to become one yet. You have some more maturing to do. In fact, it's been my observation that most men, and women for that matter, do a lot of their maturing after they are married, and even more once they have children. Even though I don't expect you to have each and every one of these traits completely right now, it seems to me they would be excellent characteristics for a man who wants to lead his family in a godly manner. As I share some thoughts about them, you be thinking about

# Jeff McLean: His Courtship

where you stand in that characteristic. Does it accurately describe you? If not, what changes need to be made in your life? Let the Holy Spirit speak to you. My prayer is that He would also speak to me as to where I need to make changes."

Jeff grabbed a pencil and Mom's kitchen notebook and jotted down notes as Dad talked. He had a feeling that these were going to be things that he would want to study and meditate about. And he was right!

"A leader, and that is what you will be as a husband, should be blameless. He should be above reproach, even from the non-Christian folks who know him. This is one of those things that is hard to get but easy to lose. It really speaks to your reputation. What do people say about you when you're not around? That's a tough one, isn't it?" Dad asked.

"It sure is, because there's no way to hide. It's not what you say you believe, but how you actually live that is going to determine if you are considered blameless by the people around you," Jeff answered.

"That's right," Dad agreed. "Let's look at a few more characteristics. A godly leader should not be self-willed, should not be soon angry, not given to wine, and not a striker. He should also not be controlled or ruled by the desire for money, regardless of whether he uses good or bad methods. He should also have obedient children and be the husband of one wife."

"I shouldn't have any trouble with those last two," Jeff laughed. "Since I don't have a wife or children."

Dad grinned. "I agree. But how could those relate in your situation?"

Jeff thought for a moment before answering. "I

suppose I should be committed to disciplining any children that the Lord might bless me with."

"Right," Dad said. "And you should be equally committed to be the husband of only one wife. You know that God hates divorce, yet you also know that the Bible says that he who even looks at a woman with lust in his mind, has committed adultery with her already in his heart. What I'm saying is that a godly leader for a home shouldn't even let his eyes wander when another woman walks by. Do you understand what I mean?"

"Yes, sir, I do," Jeff answered gravely. "That's hard, isn't it, Dad?" This was beginning to be a very frank and open discussion.

"Yes, it is. And it can only be done with the help of the Holy Spirit. But it can be done."

Both men paused and let those words sink in a little bit. Then Dad continued, "A godly leader should be a lover of hospitality. That word means more than just serving those who happen to stop at your doorstep. It actually means soliciting the opportunity to show hospitality."

"So, it's not good enough just to say your home is available to anyone who stops by, but then you always keep the lights off and the gate locked," Jeff noted.

"Exactly," Dad said. "Titus 1:10 also says that a godly leader should be a lover of good men. Who do you wish to spend your time with? Those who might be non-Christians but who you just prefer to be around because they are funny, or knowledgeable about certain things, like how to weld aluminum and stainless steel together? Or do you wish to spend your time with men who love and trust God, even though they might not be as entertaining or helpful in your occupation? That's really something to think about for all of us.

"The Bible also says that a godly man should be sober. That doesn't just mean to not be drunk with alcohol. It means here to be self controlled as to opinion or passion. Temperate would be another way to put it. Do you have to tell everyone every opinion you have? Do you have to let everyone else know your emotions or passion on every issue? If so, you're really not displaying soberness."

"I've read these verses before," Jeff remarked as his dad paused. "But I somehow never thought they would apply to a man seeking marriage. Now I do, though. If a man wants to lead his family, he needs these traits."

"No one will have all of them perfectly," Dad suggested. "However, every man who desires marriage should be working on them with the power of the Holy Spirit. Let's see what other characteristics are important. The man should be just. I believe the Greek word means innocent. It also means equitable in character or action. How could someone be just?"

"I suppose by giving your employer an honest day's work," Jeff suggested. "Also, not showing partiality. You know, like thinking that everything Mary does is okay, just because she's a friend, but thinking that nothing that Larry does is okay, because I don't like him."

"Right," Dad praised. "I think it also involves the desire to remain innocent. A man shouldn't try out bad things, even once, just to experience them. I've known of men who never intended to frequent bars, yet felt it was okay to go to a bar once just to see what it was like.  That's not trying to remain innocent."

"I see what you mean," Jeff said.  "Most people seem to think that it's okay for boys just to sow a few wild oats.  But God says we will reap what we sow."

Dad continued looking at the Titus 1 passage.  "A godly leader should hold fast the faithful word as he has been taught and be able to convince those who oppose him."

"I remember you talking about that during our family prayer time last week," Jeff commented.  "You said that it was important for you to teach us, so that we would actually have something to hold fast to.  You also said that we can expect many gainsayers, or people who oppose our beliefs, in our lives and that we should be ready to defend our beliefs from Scripture."

"That's right," Dad beamed.  It was encouraging that his lessons were sinking in.  "A godly man should obviously be able to feed his flock, according to 1 Peter 5.  In a husband's role, his flock would be his wife and children.  It is the father's responsibility to teach his family.  A man should not depend on pastors, or youth groups, or books, or anything else to teach his family.  That's the father's job.  The passage also emphasizes that he teach by example.  So, a man who is trying to see if he is ready to get married should see if his life, right now as a bachelor, is the right kind of example."

"Sure," Jeff noted.  "If you're not living the right kind of example now, chances are that you won't make that many changes once you get married."

Dad got up and put a few more logs on the fire.

# Jeff McLean: His Courtship

"A godly leader should be humble. We've talked many times about the importance of not being puffed up with pride, and how that is 180° different from what the world is teaching us. In fact, I believe we should find ways in which to reduce the pride we have and prevent more from arising."

"Things like always giving God the glory for what we have accomplished," Jeff asked. "And not calling attention to the things we have done."

"Right," Dad agreed. "Again, that's hard to do. We basically have to unlearn what the world has been teaching us in that area. The Bible also says that a godly leader should be vigilant, because the devil is on the prowl, seeking whom he will devour. That suggests that the man should not only be awake to the possibility of such an attack, but also be watchful for any attack from Satan that might come his way. Of course, the only way to ward off such attacks is by the power of God."

Dad looked at Jeff. "Here's a characteristic that you meet for sure. It says that a godly leader should not be a new convert. Since you have been a Christian for years, and have steadily grown in your faith, you are eligible to lead your family in that regard. New Christians, however, probably need time to mature before they enter into courtship.

"Holy. That one-word characteristic of a godly leader mentioned in Titus 1 sums up much of what we've been talking about," Dad concluded. "To be holy is to be spiritually perfect or pure. None of us will ever reach that mark in this world. Yet, it should be our goal, and with God's help we should be striving for it each day."

# Jeff McLean: His Courtship

"You've mentioned a lot of traits, Dad," Jeff sighed, looking at the list he had jotted down. "I definitely need to work on a number of them."

"I know you do, son," Dad said gently. "So do I. I feel that God wants us to be working hard on each of these things." He looked at Jeff carefully. "I've been studying your life for some time now, Jeff. In my opinion, you are ready to move ahead in courtship as the Lord leads you to. Let's pray that God would help us in this endeavor."

Both men bowed their heads and prayed earnestly for a time. When they rose to their feet, Jeff felt closer to his dad than he ever had in his life. "Thanks, Dad for being the best father a man could ever want."

Tears were in Dad's eyes. "Thank you, Jeff, for being such a good son. May God bless you on this new voyage in your life." With that, both men walked out and finished the morning chores.

# Chapter Five

At lunch, Jeff felt a happiness and joy that he hadn't experienced for a long time. *How can things get better?* he asked himself. Dad was in a particularly good mood and told of several happy times when he was a boy.

"You sure are smiling a lot, Jeff," Mom said, noticing her oldest son. "What's your secret?"

"For one thing, it sure is a fine day," Jeff commented. "Also, I haven't even been chased by a bull this morning!"

Everyone laughed, remembering the episode back in early October.

Janet spoke up. "That reminds me," she said. "I've gotten several letters from my pen pal from upstate that I forgot to share with you. Do you all want to hear them?" Everyone said "Yes," so she ran and grabbed a few letters. The first one, which was dated several months back, read:

Dear Janet,

It was so good to get your letter and learn more about your farm. Before I forget, Nancy told me to tell you that I borrowed one of her dresses last week. So, I guess she and I are both guilty of borrowing each other's clothes now. . .

Oh, I just can't imagine having a big bull chasing me,

like you described in your letter.  Everyone here sat on the edge of their seats as I read your letter.  Is your brother Jeff okay now?  I hope so.  We prayed for him.  And Luke was SO brave!  I know you're glad to have such a brave brother-in-law.

It was neat to read how Sarah's courtship worked out. I pray that God would help me have wisdom whenever I move into that phase of my life.  It's such a big decision!  Do you ever get afraid thinking about how important it is, and what if you make a bad decision? I do!  But I'm praying, asking God to help me trust Him even in that.

I've started volunteering my time at a nursing home at the edge of our town.  It's a lot of work, but I just love it.  I'm thankful God has given me health and energy and I want to share it with those in need.  Do you do any kind of volunteer work?

I got some new fish.  One is called a Bala Shark and looks, of course, just like a tiny shark.  . . .

Please write soon.  In Christ,  Lisa

P.S.  I've finally memorized Romans 8! (Thanks for your prayers about that ☺)  Do you memorize large sections of Scripture or just verses?  I've tried both and really like memorizing the longer passages.

That evening Dad talked to Mom about his conversation with Jeff.  She had been expecting Jeff to move in that direction for some time, so it didn't

# Jeff McLean: His Courtship

exactly come as a shock. Still, she was a little sad, as only a mom can be, to think of her son growing up and moving away to start his own life. "We've talked about possible candidates for Jeff's courtship over the last several years," Mom said. "Do you have any new ideas? Did Jeff mention anyone he is thinking about?"

"No, I'm afraid I have no new ideas. It seems that anyone we know who is committed to courtship would be too young for him right now," Dad replied. "And no, Jeff didn't mention anyone."

"What about Colleen Paralet?" Mom asked.

"I don't think so," Dad answered. "She and her parents have told everyone that they are committed to courtship. Yet, it's not uncommon to see her flirting with young men at church almost every week. It's like you said once, Kate, many people say they are committed to courtship, but then go ahead and act like they're not. I'm more impressed by results than words."

"Me too," Mom agreed. "I guess we'll just have to wait on the Lord to bring someone into his life. Like we did for Sarah."

"That's true," Dad said. He was a little restless and kept adjusting his pillow.

"Okay, you're thinking about something," Mom said. "I've been married to you long enough to know that you've got something on your mind."

Dad laughed. "Can't hide anything from you, can I? I'm not sure I should even mention it, it seems so far-fetched."

Mom didn't beg. She knew if Dad wanted to tell her that he would.

"It really is rather silly of me, I'm sure," Dad

began. "But maybe it's the Lord who is putting this person in my head. I guess time will tell."

Again Mom didn't speak. Finally, Dad said, "For some reason I was impressed with the letter that Janet's pen pal wrote. I guess what impressed me the most is that she is memorizing Scripture. You just don't hear of that many young people trying to memorize Scripture today. But whether she would be a good candidate for Jeff, I couldn't begin to say. I've only heard Janet read a few letters from her. I'm probably just trying to find Jeff someone soon. He's such a good boy."

Mom gave him a hug. "Yes, he's such a good boy. And you're such a good dad. I don't know anything about her, either. I could write Lisa's mom if you want me to, and try to get to know her."

"Let's give it a little time yet," Dad said after thinking about it for a minute. "Let's pray and see if we get any direction."

They did pray about the matter, but didn't feel any particular direction one way or the other. A few days later, Dad confided, "Kate, you feel free to introduce yourself to Lisa's mom by writing her a letter. But please don't mention anything about Jeff or the possibility of a courtship."

"I agree," Mom said. "We'll just see what happens. It's really in the Lord's hands."

# Chapter Six

Over the next month and  a half, Mom exchanged letters with Joan Harris, Lisa's mom.  They hit it off right away, having many of the same interests and opinions.  When Gerald, Lisa's father, enclosed a note to Dad with one letter, that started a correspondence between the two men.  Dad seemed impressed with what he learned about Gerald.  Gerald had written a short article for one of the Christian men's magazines, and after securing a copy, Dad found that he had a lot in common with the man.

No one mentioned anything in any of the letters about courtship.  After more prayer, Dad felt led to call Gerald and broach the subject.  To his surprise, Gerald had been thinking along those lines himself and encouraged more conversation and prayer about the matter.  Now, the parents exchanged a number of phone calls, letters, and pictures.  There was even talk of a possible personal visit, although schedules didn't allow it yet.

Jeff gradually got the full strength back in his arm and worked in earnest on his farm.  There was a spring in his step even though a casual observer would be hard pressed to see any real progress taking place.  The counsel he had received was true;  it was going to go slowly and take a lot of time.  Yet, Jeff's responsibility was to continue working away at it.

Friends continued to help.  In late March, Luke surprised Jeff by informing him that they were coming for  a week-long visit at the McLeans' house.  The

# Jeff McLean: His Courtship

primary purpose of the visit was so that Luke could lend his expert carpentry skills to whatever tasks Jeff assigned him.

It was so good to visit with Luke and his family again. Sarah enjoyed spending lots of time with Mom, talking through many of the issues surrounding child raising and being a godly wife and mother. It was fun for everyone to play with baby Noah, Sarah's latest little bundle of joy.

As one topic led into another, Mom was reminded of something she had meant to ask. "Sarah, would you like to join a buying club I'm starting? I know you do like to buy grain and grind your own flour. If you join this club, I can save you money on the grain. Also, it's organic, which is hard to find in large quantities where you live."

Sarah was excited. "That sounds great. We could pick up our order when we visit you. I'll tell Luke what we're doing. But I'm sure he won't have any problem with it."

Later that evening, Sarah spoke to her mother in low tones as she helped Mom wash the dishes. "Mom, I need you to talk to Luke for me. I told him about the buying club, but he said he wasn't interested. He said he didn't think we had storage space for the larger quantities that the club would require us to buy at one time. Also, he didn't think that our budget would allow us to spend so much on a single item. Isn't that strange? I'm sure if you talk to him, you can convince him to change his mind. After all, we need to get organic wheat at a good price."

Mom finished rinsing and drying the dish that Sarah handed to her. "I don't think I should," she

# Jeff McLean: His Courtship

finally said.

"Why not?" Sarah was perplexed. Then, thinking that Mom didn't want to appear to oppose her son-in-law's leadership, she commented, "At least help me come up with some good arguments to present to Luke. You and I both know this is something that we shouldn't pass up!"

"Sarah, I can't do that either," Mom began. "I believe you need to be submissive to Luke's decisions and wishes."

"Well sure, Mom, I agree. I know I should be submissive to Luke, and with God's help I'm trying to do just that. But in this case, I don't think he waited to hear me out. It's like he just made a decision without all of the facts. I'm not sure it's appropriate submitting to Luke when he makes bad decisions like this."

Mom was visibly shaken. "Sit down, Sarah," she said. "I need to talk to you a little bit. No, don't worry about the dishes. Just have a seat."

When Sarah was seated at the table, Mom continued. "Sarah, God calls us to be submissive to our husbands. The Bible does not say that we are to be submissive whenever we agree with their decision or think they really listened to us. Let's see what the Scriptures say."

Mom reached for the Bible that was kept on a small table in the kitchen, then opened it to I Peter 3. "Listen carefully to the fifth and sixth verses, Sarah. 'For after this manner in the old time the holy women also, who trusted in God, adorned themselves, being in subjection unto their own husbands: Even as Sarah obeyed Abraham, calling him lord: whose daughters ye

59

# Jeff McLean: His Courtship

are, as long as ye do well, and are not afraid with any amazement.'" Mom looked up, her eyes resting gently on Sarah.

"Daughters of Sarah. That's what God wants us to be. By nature, we are daughters of Eve — wanting to persuade our husbands, wanting knowledge and decision-making ability. But when we are following our own sinful natures, then Satan can come to us and deceive us. That fruit looked just as good and innocent to Eve as this buying club does to you."

Sarah was silent for a moment, looking at the pattern of flowers on the tablecloth. "But Mom," she began slowly, "what about the verse that says men are to love their wives just as Christ loved the church and gave Himself for it? Shouldn't Luke want to please me and try to let me do things that aren't harmful?"

Mom waited for Sarah to meet her eyes. When Sarah continued to look at the tablecloth, Mom said her name in a serious tone. "Sarah." Finally, Sarah looked at Mom's face. "Honey, let's look that verse up. It is in Ephesians, chapter five I think." Mom set the Bible in front of her eldest daughter. "Look it up please."

Sarah turned to the page and read it aloud. "'Husbands, love your wives, even as Christ also loved the church, and gave himself for it.'"

"Who is the verse written to?" Mom asked. "It is written to the husband, not the wife. It is not our business to teach our husbands how they should love us. God Himself is the only one who has that responsibility. He may use many means to accomplish that, but nowhere in Scripture does He give the job to wives. As a matter of fact, Paul teaches in I Timothy

2:12 that women are not to teach their husbands anything."

Mom sat quietly. Then she laughed softly, and at Sarah's questioning look explained, "I was just thinking back. Some years ago, when I was a new Christian and struggling with this issue, I used to have to remind myself, 'How can your husband hear God if you're always preaching at him?'"

Sarah laughed with her mother. "I do want to be a good wife, and adorn myself with a meek and quiet spirit, as Sarah did. But it can be hard to let go of my own ideas. Especially when they seem to be really *good* ideas, and I disagree with Luke's decision."

Nodding, Mom pulled the Bible back toward herself. "I understand. But let's look up one more verse. Listen to Ephesians 5:22, which is just a few verses above the one we women like to read, but which is really written to our husbands! Verse 22 reads, 'Wives, submit yourselves unto your own husbands, as unto the Lord.' As unto the Lord. That is the key, Sarah. Our husbands aren't the Lord, obviously. They aren't perfect, and they don't make perfect decisions. The Lord would never ask us to sin, so we are not to sin in order to submit to our husbands. We are, however, to submit to them as though we were submitting unto the Lord. If Jesus asked us to do anything, even something very hard, most of us would say we were willing to obey Him."

Sarah nodded, then her mother continued. "Well, Jesus has asked us to do something. He has asked us to submit to our husbands as though we were submitting unto Him. Are we going to obey Him?"

Sarah drew a deep breath, then smiled at Mom. "I

think I'll just keep buying those wonderful little five-pound bags of wheat at the health-food store."

"That's my Sarah!" exclaimed Mom.


The visit of the Williams came to a close and everyone said goodbye. "Wow, we got a lot done when Luke was here!" Jeff commented. "Imagine what we could get done if he lived right next door."

"Don't forget that he is a professional carpenter, and would have to spend most of his time making money to support his family," Dad reminded him. "But it is nice to see you two work together and get a lot done. You probably don't realize how much it means to your mom and me to see how well everyone gets along with Luke." After a second, he continued. "Which sort of brings up a subject that I have been meaning to talk to you about for a while. I know you would like to find a wife. Has the Lord shown you any possible candidates yet?"

"Not really, Dad. I'm hoping that something will happen, though," Jeff replied candidly.

"Your mom and I have someone that we think you ought to at least possibly consider. If you want to learn more about her just let me know."

"Of course I do!" Jeff exploded. "Who is it?"

Dad seemed a little hesitant. "We've never met her before, Jeff, so I don't want to sound like we are endorsing her or anything like that. But we have been talking with her parents and feel they are truly godly folks. At least as much as you can learn about someone by talking with them on the phone and through the mail."

Jeff was getting exasperated. "Dad, who *is* it?"

# Jeff McLean: His Courtship

"Well, it's that pen pal of Janet's," Dad finally explained. "Her name is Lisa Harris." Dad watched closely for Jeff's reaction when Lisa's name was mentioned. Jeff merely smiled.

"I remember Janet reading some letters from her. Seems like I also remember Janet saying how great her family was. To be honest with you, Dad, I somewhat discounted what Janet said. She thinks just about everyone's family is great, if you know what I mean."

Dad agreed. "True. But, like I said, we have been having some interesting conversations with Gerald and Joan Harris. In fact, we would like to get together and meet them." Then he quickly added, "Whether you decide to court Lisa or not, that is. We would just like to get to know them."

Jeff removed his hat and rubbed the back of his neck. "When are they coming?"

Dad laughed. "Not for supper tonight, don't worry! Actually, we have been trying to schedule a get-together for several weeks now, but it never seems to work out." Dad looked at Jeff seriously. "I don't want to sound like we are trying to influence you toward Lisa. Like I said, we don't really know her."

"That's okay," Jeff said. "I'm open to whoever the Lord might bring into my path. I would enjoy meeting her and learning more about her."

"Well, we'll just have to see if that's going to be possible," Dad concluded. "In the meantime, I'll share with you some of the letters and pictures we've received as well as tell you about the conversations we've had."

Jeff continued to work on his farm. By now, most who drove by Jeff's farm could note changes in the place.  Luke and Sarah came for a weekend visit in mid-April and Jeff was thankful for some more of Luke's expertise.  On Saturday, the two men replaced four major rafters in the barn that Jeff had been worrying about for some time.  Sarah stopped by with some bolts that she had picked up from the hardware store for them.  "Oh, come look at these, guys!" she exclaimed to Luke and Jeff as she walked toward the barn.  They stopped what they were doing and walked to where Sarah was standing near the house.

"Look at the beautiful tulips coming up!" she said. "I had no idea you had tulips here, Jeff."  Then looking around the farm, she continued, "This really can be made into a beautiful place.  It has real potential!"

"I sure hope so, sister," Jeff replied, laughing.  "Of course, I suppose it's going to be mine whether it has any potential or not."

"Oh!" Sarah scolded.  "It really is going to be pretty.  Look at the way those trees will offer shade. Why, you could plant impatiens under there.  And over there, under those maple trees, see that cute stone wall that is . . . well, it's kind of all fallen down?"  Jeff laughed.

"Don't you laugh at me, Jeff McLean," Sarah said with a smile.  "With just a little work that can be made into one of the most beautiful spots on the whole farm."  Her eyes were shining.  "Yes, this place has real potential."

# Chapter Seven

As the weeks passed, the McLeans and Harrises continued to write letters and carry on phone conversations. Everything sounded very positive to all parties. Dad had the opportunity to talk to Lisa and seemed impressed with her gentle, quiet spirit. The Harrises had carefully broached the subject of courtship with Lisa and she had been open to seeing what might happen. Of course, absolutely nothing was certain until Jeff and Lisa had a chance to meet and learn more about each other. However, Jeff was impressed with what he had learned about Lisa. *She just might be the one*, he thought.

Both families set aside the second weekend in May as a time when they could finally meet each other. Tentatively, the plan called for the Harrises to drive down to the McLean farm. Although the other children in each family weren't made aware of the possibility of a courtship, they were all excited about the upcoming visit. Of course, Janet was nearly beside herself with anticipation of finally meeting her newest pen-pal.

Soon the wet, cool spring, along with the inevitable mud that went with it, was replaced with the warmer weather of early summer. The family's favorite summer birds returned to their nesting areas on the farm. Apple trees began to blossom. A number of new calves were born. Summer, with all of its busyness, was definitely on its way.

On a warm, early May day things changed at the

# Jeff McLean: His Courtship

McLeans' home.  It all happened so quickly, as these things usually do.  There was no time for preparation. Janet suddenly started vomiting right after the lunch meal.  She also complained of a pain in her side.  At first no one was alarmed.  Then she started running a fever.  Medicines didn't seem to be able to bring the fever down.  At the emergency room it was determined that Janet had a serious case of appendicitis.

"It looks like her appendix has already ruptured," the doctor said quickly.  "We need to operate right away."

After surgery, the doctors reported that Janet went through the operation fine.  However, they stated that her recovery would take a good deal of time.

After her stitches were removed five days later, Janet seemed much improved.  A few days later she was released from the hospital.  The doctors suggested that Janet take it easy for several weeks while the various layers of tissue in the abdominal wall healed. It was important that she have a quiet and restful environment.  Mom promised the doctors to do everything she could to insure Janet peace and quiet.

After Janet was home and resting comfortably in bed, Dad remembered the planned visit of the Harrises.  "I better call them right now and let them know what's going on," he said to Mom.

Mrs. Harris understood completely and said that they would be remembering Janet in their prayers.  "Is there anything else we can do?" she asked.

"I'm afraid not," Dad answered.  "But thanks for asking.  Just pray that we would have the strength to get everything done that needs doing around here. With Janet out of the picture, it will be especially hard to get the garden in, and keep up with all of the many things that we have to do around here in the early summer. Many of our friends have already offered to help. We'll be fine."

That evening, the phone rang. "It's for you, Dad," Steve said, running into the living room with the news. "It's Mr. Harris."

"Hello, Gerald," Dad said as he picked up the phone. "How big was *your* long distance phone bill last month?"

Mr. Harris laughed. The men had been comparing phone bills for the last two months as the families continued to get acquainted with each other. "It wasn't *too* bad," Mr. Harris returned. "Say, Joan was telling me about Janet. We're sorry and will keep her in our prayers."

"Thanks. She's going to be okay. She just needs some time to rest and recover, according to the doctors."

"I'm sure that's true," Mr. Harris replied. "Which is partly why I'm calling. I know your family is going to have a lot to do around there over the next several weeks. Well . . . what I'm proposing is this. What if we loaned Lisa to you for a couple of weeks? She could do all of the housework and even help in the garden. That way Kate wouldn't have to worry about how Janet's jobs are going to get done. What do you say?"

Dad didn't know what to say. "I . . . I don't know, Gerald. That would be a pretty big sacrifice on your part. I'm sure you have many things that Lisa needs to do around your house."

Mr. Harris laughed. "You mean, take care of her

sixteen-year-old sister? No, our situation is different from yours, David. We no longer have any little ones around the place. And Nancy, along with Joan, can take care of all the household kinds of things here." He paused. "I'm not trying to force her on you, of course. I'm just offering to bring her down if that would be a help to your family."

"I really appreciate that," Dad said. "Let me talk to Kate and think about it. I'll call you back later tonight. Is that okay?"

"No problem. I'm usually up until 11:00 or 11:30, anyway," Mr. Harris responded. "And it really won't be any problem for us. Just remember that."

"Thanks," Dad said sincerely.

After talking it over with Mom, Dad decided that it would be very helpful to have Lisa visit and help around the house. Dad hadn't even realized all of the things that needed doing in the next several weeks. So, later that evening he called Mr. Harris back and said that they would really appreciate having Lisa as a helper.

"We can drive her down tomorrow morning," Mr. Harris said. "She was hoping you would say yes."

"Well, we really appreciate it," Dad said. "And don't worry, we'll take good care of her. I'll make sure she is always properly chaperoned."

"I'm not worrying about that," Mr. Harris responded. "I think I know you well enough already, just by talking with you on the phone to know that. It will be good to finally meet you and your family."

The two finished their conversation, discussing the details of the visit. Mom was relieved to hear how the conversation had gone. "She is really going to be a blessing," she said.

"Yes, and we'll get to learn more about her as a potential mate for Jeff, also," Dad replied.  "Isn't it interesting how God can use situations, even like these, for our good?"

# Chapter Eight

Everyone was excited the next morning when the plans were announced at the breakfast table. Janet, when she learned of the Harris' visit, was the only one concerned. "Mom, it sounds like they will be here for two meals. That's going to be a lot of work for you to prepare and I can't do a thing to help."

"Don't be silly," Mom responded. "Remember, they are coming to help, not be in the way or be entertained. You just rest. And soon you'll get to meet your pen pal!"

"I can hardly wait," Janet enthused.

At about 10:30 a small van pulled into the McLeans' driveway. "What do they look like?" Rachel asked Becky.

"Girls, don't stare out of the window!" Mom said, who had been walking past at the time. "Let's go out and meet them."

Everyone was happy to finally meet. In a way, it seemed as though the families already knew each other. There wasn't that hesitancy that sometimes happens when you meet a new family. Of course, it was made somewhat easier since there were no younger children in the Harris household for the McLean children to be "shy" of. Dad encouraged everyone to come inside and meet Janet.

Before long, Mom was calling everyone to be seated for the noon meal. After the blessing, the conversation continued. There were so many little things to learn about each other. Things that you wouldn't necessarily talk about in letters or on long distance phone calls. Things such as where they had lived in their lives, what books they enjoyed, funny things that had happened, and so forth. Lunchtime finished before the questions were all asked or answered.

It was clear that the families were getting along well together. Nancy took an interest in Rachel and Becky and offered to show them how to crochet. Mrs. Harris and Mom seemed a lot alike in their tastes in furniture and furnishings. Even though Mr. Harris was a manager at a company and not a farmer, he and Dad had some interesting conversations about the economy and where the federal government was heading. Jeff asked Lisa a few questions and was pleased with her gentle, quiet voice.

After lunch, Mr. Harris stood up and said, "I'd like to see your farm, if you wouldn't mind showing me."

"Sure, that would be no problem," Dad said. "I can show you around. Then, maybe Steve and Ben will have to give you any detailed tours you would like. I'm afraid I really need to spread some manure this afternoon. With Janet's sickness I've gotten behind and need to get this on the fields before the hay starts growing too much."

As the men started leaving the room, Mrs. Harris asked, "Can we all come? I'm sure Lisa and Nancy would also like to see your place. Being in the city, they don't get much chance to see how things work on a farm."

"I'd be glad to take all of you along," Dad smiled. "Of course, there might be a little bit more dirt than you're used to, but the Lord has blessed us with a very pretty place."

After all of the Harrises left the room, Mom, Rachel, and Becky began to clear the table. "Mom, why aren't they going to help us do the dishes?" Becky asked.

"Shhh," Mom said. "They might hear you."

"But we have so many dishes to clear and wash," Rachel added. "We always help other people when we visit at their house."

"I know," Mom said. "That's because we want to help. We are a large family and we don't want to be a burden on other families when we eat there."

"Yes," Becky understood. "But even if they aren't a large family, they still should have offered to help. Shouldn't they?"

Mom didn't know how to respond. "All I can say is that I hope you would always volunteer. Let's not think about what the Harrises did or didn't do. Let's just focus on what we need to do. Okay?" With that, everyone started working on the dishes.

The Harris family was impressed with the farm. They couldn't seem to believe the size of the cattle when they were close to them. "They look sort of small out standing in a field," Mrs. Harris said. She was frightened of them.

Mr. Harris used the small amount of time he had on this visit asking Jeff questions and learning more about what kind of a man he was. Even though Jeff hadn't said anything about a desire to court his daughter yet, he still wanted to learn what he could while he had such an easy opportunity.

"What are your dreams, Jeff?" he asked. "I mean,

# Jeff McLean: His Courtship

what do you hope to be when you're, say, thirty years old?"

"A little wiser," was Jeff's quick reply. Everyone laughed. "I wasn't trying to be funny, Mr. Harris," he said. "It's just that I intend to be a farmer the rest of my life, and by thirty, I do hope to not be making the mistakes I'm making right now."

"Well put," Mr. Harris reflected. "Well put."

"Did I hear that you already own your own farm?" Mrs. Harris asked.

"Well, yes and no," was Jeff's reply. He then explained the nature of the agreement he had with Mrs. Walters.

"Still, I'd say that's doing pretty well for a young man who just turned twenty-three years old. You must be very proud of him, David."

Dad chose his words carefully. "I am very thankful for the way the Lord has blessed Jeff," he responded. "I think he has a very bright future ahead of him."

The rest of the afternoon was spent in various ways. Dad and Jeff worked on cleaning out the loafing shed and spreading manure, while Mrs. Harris, Lisa, Janet, Nancy, Mom, Rachel and Becky visited. Mr. Harris wandered around the farm some, then drove down to look at Jeff's farm.

Right before supper, Mr. Harris and Dad had a private conversation on the back porch. "I'm really impressed with Jeff," Mr. Harris said. "He seems like one of the nicest young men I've met. In our conversations, I sometimes forget that he is only twenty-three. He seems older, somehow."

Dad just smiled. "Oh, Jeff's got his faults, just like

the rest of us." Then after thinking a second, he added, "They are all different, aren't they? I mean, children. Some seem to mature early, for others it seems to take longer than normal. I guess I would say that Jeff is one of those who seemed to mature very early."

"I guess so," Mr. Harris reflected. "Say, I dropped by to look at his farm." He turned his head to make sure no one could hear him. "It's got some beautiful land. But the buildings seem to be in pretty bad shape. I guess he's going to tear them down so he can build his house?"

"No, I don't think that's his plan," Dad said. "Actually, he has already been working on them for a while. You should have seen them before he did!"

Mr. Harris was silent for a moment, contemplating the facts. "Who knows?" he finally decided. "Jeff's a pretty smart young man. Maybe he can make something of those old buildings yet. Seems like a lot of work to me, though." Then, changing the subject, he talked about Lisa. "She won't need anything special while she's here. She is ready to go to work and do whatever you need her to do. I hope she can be helpful to your family."

"I'm sure she will do fine," Dad said. "She seems like a very sweet young lady to me, although I haven't had much chance to talk to her yet. This will be a good time for us to get to know her better."

"Has Jeff said anything to you about her?" Mr. Harris asked. "I mean, has he said anything about her since he's met her?"

Dad thought for a second. "I don't think he's said anything to me. But we've been pretty busy today.

# Jeff McLean: His Courtship

Besides, he hasn't had much chance to talk with her."

After supper, Lisa asked quietly, "Can I please help with the dishes, Mrs. McLean? Or is there something else you would rather have me do?"

"I think it would be most helpful if you cleared the table and swept the floor. Thanks," Mom smiled.

Before long, the Harrises were saying goodbye and heading down the driveway. Mom smiled at Lisa. "Come let me show you to your room." After getting Lisa set up, she added, "If there is anything you need, just let us know."

"Thank you, Mrs. McLean," Lisa replied. "You have been so kind. I think I'll go to bed now if that is okay with you. For some reason I'm very tired."

In the morning, Jeff noticed that Lisa was up early. "Good morning," she greeted him as he entered the kitchen. Mom was making biscuits and Lisa was setting the table.

"Good morning," Jeff returned cheerfully. Then turning to Mom he said, "I'm going to check on that heifer who was having trouble calving last night. She had her calf but it was dead. I'm afraid we're going to have some problems with the heifer today, too." Jeff lifted his hat from the nail beside the kitchen door and left the house.

"Did he say he was out there with the cow last night? He must be very tired today," Lisa commented.

"He's probably a little tired, but I think he's used to it," Mom replied. "During this time of year, he spends a lot of time helping cows that are having trouble, and just checking on them. He really cares about his animals."

"That's good," Lisa noted. "Janet was telling me

75

that you usually plant a lot of your garden about now. Is that what we are going to work on today?"

Mom thought about that for a minute. "Well, you can if you want to, Lisa. It's not the easiest job on the farm, but it does need to be done."

"I'm not afraid of hard work," Lisa responded quickly. "I enjoy our garden at home, working in our flowers and tomatoes. Actually, it sounds like fun to help put in a large garden."

"Well, okay," Mom said. "Then I'll assign Rachel and Becky to get started on the laundry and breakfast dishes after we've eaten. I'll check on Janet, work on the children's homeschool lessons, and try to find time to get out and help you every chance I can."

After breakfast, Mom instructed Lisa on how to plant potatoes. "This is going to be easy," Lisa remarked. "I don't think I'll need any help at all." With that, she bent over and began to plant the first row of potatoes.

As the morning progressed, Lisa worked hard in the garden. Mom was only able to step out and help her a few times because Samuel hurt his hand and needed her attention for a while. *That's okay*, thought Lisa. *I'm here to help. If this helps Janet and the McLeans, then I've accomplished my reason for being here. And, if I do it myself, then Jeff will see that I'm a hard worker*. She was impressed with Jeff and wanted to make a favorable impression on him.

So, Lisa continued to work. However, the temperature rose as the day wore on. She began to look at the rows and rows that still needed potatoes and got a little discouraged. It may sound silly, but it was especially frustrating to her that she couldn't keep the

# Jeff McLean: His Courtship

dirt out of her fingernails. At home, she had always worked with gloves on. Planting potatoes, however, required her to push the potato eye deep into the ground, and gloves would have been practically useless. Still, she tried to work hard and not have a complaining attitude.

*How can Jeff see what I'm doing anyway?* she asked herself a little later, scanning the farm. *He's probably off in some pasture somewhere and doesn't even know I'm doing this.* She tried to think of an innocent way in which she could let him know how hard she had worked, but couldn't think of any.

At lunch, Mom commented on how hard Lisa had worked. "I can't believe you got all of that done this morning. Are you sure you've never planted potatoes before?"

Lisa was ecstatic. She hadn't even had to bring up the subject at all. "No, I've never planted potatoes before. I just work hard at something until the job is done, that's all." Then feeling that she might have displayed a little too much pride, she added, "Besides, you are a very good teacher, Mrs. McLean." She was hoping that Jeff was paying attention.

"What does Mom have planned for you this afternoon?" Jeff asked.

"If she doesn't mind, I think I'll let her finish the potatoes," Mom answered. "Unless you're too tired, Lisa," she added quickly. "I don't want you to push yourself."

"Oh, I'm fine," Lisa replied. "I would like to finish the job since I started it." Lisa thought she hid her emotions well. It was pretty obvious that she wasn't exactly thrilled with her assigned task. She didn't say so, however.

That evening, Mom and Dad discussed the day. "How is Lisa working out?" Dad asked.

"Well, I'll have to say this for her. She did work hard planting the potatoes," Mom answered honestly. "At least she seems to be able to finish a hard job."

"That's good," Dad said. "How was her attitude?"

Mom hesitated. "I can't really say, David. I wasn't with her much today and would need more time to see. I wouldn't want to make any hasty conclusions."

"I agree," Dad said. "Jeff seems to be pretty impressed with her. At least he said he liked the way she wasn't complaining about doing the potatoes, the way Janet often does. That's all he has said to me, though. I guess he is going to give it more time, too."

# Chapter Nine

T he next morning, Tuesday, opened with clouds and the sound of thunder. It was still dark when Mom started putting together the morning's breakfast. Rachel and Becky walked sleepily into the kitchen and started setting the table. A few minutes later Steve and Ben came walking in, talking about what they hoped to do today. "Don't forget that we have math to do this morning, first," Mom reminded them.

"I think I hear Samuel," Mom spoke to Rachel. "Will you please see if he needs any help getting dressed?"

"He wouldn't listen to us, Mom," Ben informed her. "When Samuel saw that it was dark and heard the thunder, he said it was going to snow. He's up there putting on his winter clothes and trying to find some wool socks to wear." Steve laughed, and then so did Ben.

"Rachel, please see that he gets dressed for mid-May," Mom instructed.

About that time, Dad and Jeff walked in the back door. "Good morning," Dad greeted his family. "How's breakfast coming along, sweetheart?" Then before Mom could answer, he added, "Who are we missing?"

"I've seen, or at least heard, everyone up this morning, except for Lisa," Mom replied. Then a slightly worried look spread over her face. "I hope she's not sick."

"Maybe she's just tired from yesterday," Jeff commented.

"Yes, maybe so," Dad agreed. "Let's let her sleep. She'll get up when she gets up."

But a couple of hours passed and Lisa still hadn't come out of her room. Finally, Mom was too worried not to check. She quietly went outside her door and listened. Not hearing anything, she knocked gently.

"Did someone knock?" came a sleepy voice from inside.

"Yes," Mom said. "Are you all right, Lisa? It's after 9:00 and I was getting worried about you."

Movement could be heard from the other side of the door. "Yes, I'm up," Lisa reassured, trying to move quickly and quietly. She couldn't believe that she had slept so late! "I was just having my morning devotions." Mom could hear the dresser door open and close gently and the sound of Lisa dressing quickly. "I'll be there soon."

Mom quietly walked back to the kitchen. *Obviously, I woke her up and she is just now getting dressed*, she thought. *Why does she think she has to lie to me about sleeping late? She worked hard yesterday. Probably harder than she's used to. I wouldn't blame her for sleeping late. But lying . . .* That bothered Mom a lot.

Soon Lisa was in the kitchen. "I'm sorry, Mrs. McLean. I guess I got carried away with my devotions."

*Should I confront her with what I suspect?* Mom thought. *I certainly would if it were one of my children.* She decided not to, however. After all, Lisa

# Jeff McLean: His Courtship

was her guest, not her child. "I'm afraid the breakfast has all been cleared away," Mom said. "I would be happy to fix something for you, though. What would you like?"

"Oh, I'll take care of everything," Lisa assured Mom. "And clean up after myself." She had noted Mom's disturbed expression, and added, "Again, I'm sorry. The book of Acts is just too interesting, I guess."

"Yes, it is exciting," Mom agreed. Placing the pitcher of milk and several boxes of cereal on the table, Mom excused herself to go check on Janet.

A few moments later, Jeff opened the back door and called, "Is anyone in the kitchen? Hello? I need a Band-aid®. Is there anyone in there?" He didn't walk in because he had manure-covered boots on and didn't want to have to take the time to remove them.

Lisa didn't know what to do. She was afraid to say anything, because she thought Jeff might learn that she was just eating breakfast. If she was quiet, maybe he would go away.

She was relieved when the back door closed. *I guess he's given up*, she thought. *Now, if I can eat quickly and clean up, maybe no one else will notice how late I got up.*

Just then, the back door opened and Jeff came walking in quickly toward the kitchen. "Hi, Lisa, I didn't know you were in here," he greeted. He walked directly to the sink and let the water run over one of his fingers.

"Are you hurt?" Lisa asked, alarmed.

"No, not at all," Jeff laughed. "Just a cut. Happens all the time! But I always like to get even a tiny

# Jeff McLean: His Courtship

cut cleaned out and a Band-aid® covering it to keep out the germs while I work. I usually have some in my wallet, but apparently I ran out." He noticed that she was eating breakfast, but didn't say anything about it. "How are you doing this morning?"

Lisa didn't know what to say. *Should I tell him that I don't feel well? At least that would be an excuse for not getting up early.* Without thinking further, she said, "I'm fine. I was feeling a little dizzy this morning, and thought it would be best to stay in bed until the dizziness went away. I wanted to get over it quickly so I could work hard around the house this morning for your family." *That sounded pretty convincing*, she told herself.

"I didn't know you were dizzy," Mom interjected, entering the room. She had heard Lisa's conversation. "I'm sorry that you were. Are you okay now, or do you think you need to go back to bed?"

Lisa wasn't sure what to say. She felt that Mom knew that she was lying, but could hardly confess. Not with Jeff standing there. So, she just replied, a little coolly, "I'm fine now. But Jeff needs a Band-aid®."

Mom handed Jeff a Band-aid® and looked at Lisa who resumed eating breakfast. She tried not to show her disappointment.

After breakfast, Mom assigned Lisa the task of helping with the laundry. The threat of thunderstorms seemed to have moved out, although it was still partly cloudy. "I think we'll hang out the clothes this morning," Mom decided cheerfully. "The weatherman says it's supposed to turn sunny and warm this afternoon."

As Lisa hung the laundry to dry, her eyes were

# Jeff McLean: His Courtship

scanning the buildings and fields around the farm. *I wonder where everyone is working today?* she thought. It was quite humid and hot. Even though she usually enjoyed hanging out laundry at her house, there was more to do than she had ever done before. Mosquitos started bothering her, too. *I hope that Jeff is noticing what I'm doing*, she thought. She decided that if she started singing, maybe that would attract attention to her. She thought for a few minutes about some good songs to sing and chose some that she felt would sound especially pleasing.

"It is nice to hear you singing," Becky said, walking up behind Lisa. Lisa, startled, spun around to see who had addressed her.

Becky got shy at the sudden attention. "I like to hear you sing," she repeated. "But I don't know that song. What does it mean in the song when you sang, 'may your thoughts banish sadness'?"

Lisa smiled at Becky and repeated the words of the verse she had just sung:

"O let your soul now be filled with gladness, Your heart redeemed, rejoice indeed!
O may the thought banish all your sadness That in His blood you have been freed,
That God's unfailing love is yours, That you the only Son were given,
That by His death He has opened heaven, That you are ransomed as you are.

"That verse tells us that we should be glad and rejoice. We have no reason to be sad because we are Christians. God loved us so much that he gave Jesus Christ

# Jeff McLean: His Courtship

to die for our sins. Since we have been saved by
Jesus' death, we are going to heaven. Isn't that a
beautiful song?"

"Yes," Becky agreed.

"It's hard to imagine how God would send His son
to die for my sins. And I have many sins. But He did,
Becky. I need to rejoice in that fact more often than
I do. I'm afraid I worry too much about what isn't
going right instead of just thanking God for what He
has already done."

Becky started helping Lisa hang the laundry. Lisa
suddenly felt fresh and clean. *Father, forgive me for
my sins,* she prayed silently. *I do want to please You
with my life. Help me to trust in You for all things
and realize that You have prepared a place in heaven
for me. Let Your will be done in my life and help me
to accept that Holy and Perfect will. Amen.*

# Chapter Ten

O ver the next several days, Lisa tried to work hard and not complain.   It was difficult for  her, however.   *These people do nothing but work!* she thought.   Although she had brought along several books to read, she almost never had time to read the way she was accustomed to doing at home.   *Maybe that's just the way it is on a farm, especially with a big family,* she mused.   That made her start thinking about what it might be like should she marry Jeff.   *Life would be different.   Very different.*

Jeff and Dad finished the fencing project they were working on.   Now they were spending their days working on machinery in anticipation of the upcoming hay season.   The haybine, the machine that cuts and prepares the hay, needed a new chain installed.   They thought the rake wouldn't need any work, but when they began to look it over carefully, they noticed that one tire wouldn't hold air and a number of the teeth had been damaged or broken off in the last season.   Several of the hay wagons had rotting boards, as always, that needed replacing.   A lot of work.   Still, it was exciting to get everything ready and in good shape.   All too many farmers simply pull into the fields with their implements, only to learn too late about repairs that are desperately needed.   Dad wouldn't let such a thing happen, if he could help it.

On Thursday, as Jeff was removing a safety shield off the haybine, a bolt broke off.   "There's one we are going to have to replace," he said.   "Given its location,

# Jeff McLean: His Courtship

we'll have to weld a new nut onto the frame. Now a simple job becomes a much more complex one."

Dad laughed. "Isn't that the way it always seems to go? And then, if you are thinking that a repair job is going to take a long time, sometimes it isn't as bad as you first thought. Just goes to show that you never know what you're going to get into, until you really start working on that part."

"That's true," Jeff agreed. "A lot of things in life are that way. You can't always predict what things are going to be like."

It was silent for a while, then Dad spoke. "Have you had a chance to observe Lisa much?" Dad didn't want to push Jeff, but he was curious as to what his son thought of their guest.

Jeff poured some Liquid Wrench® onto several bolts he was trying to remove. The liquid was supposed to help free frozen, rusted bolts. He was going to keep from breaking off any more bolts if at all possible. "Sure, I've noticed some things about her," he said. "What do you mean?"

"Nothing," Dad commented. "I was just interested to know what your thoughts were."

Jeff thought for a minute as the liquid worked on the bolts. "She seems like a nice young lady to me. I like the way she speaks in a quiet voice. She seems to have been doing whatever Mom asked her to do. Whether she is doing them with a good attitude or not, I don't know. Mom would probably know."

Dad and Mom had held several counsels together about that topic, but before he had time to bring it up, Jeff continued speaking.

"I did hear her seem to talk a little . . . I don't

# Jeff McLean: His Courtship

know how to put it," Jeff said. "Maybe a little conde-scending to Steve yesterday. I don't know what it was all about, but Steve seemed a little hurt." He paused. "This is really hard, Dad," Jeff said. "I mean, thinking of courting and getting married is a very big responsi-bility! More than I'm afraid I ever realized. We're not talking about deciding on someone to go to town with. We're talking about 'until death do ye part.'"

"That's so true," Dad agreed. "I think it would be good for the two of you to have more time to talk. We've been so busy and she has kept so busy that there hasn't been much of a chance for you two to learn about each other. Maybe after supper, we can all go out on the porch and just relax for a change. I would like to get to know her better myself." He smiled at his eldest son. "They are predicting rain anyway, so we couldn't work much."

Jeff laughed. He knew how goal-oriented Dad was and that he wanted to get his machinery in good working condition. Still, Dad was willing to put that aside because he thought it was in Jeff's best interest.

"That sounds good. And Dad, if you think it's wise, I'd like for Lisa to see my farm," Jeff told his dad. "I think she should see where I am planning to live and what it looks like." With that, he picked up a socket wrench and slowly started pulling the handle. There was a long screech before another bolt broke off under the strain. "Well, we might as well keep the welder out. Looks like we're going to need it for several bolts today."

That evening after supper, Dad mentioned that it would be a good night to sit on the back porch. "The mosquitos don't seem to be too bad tonight." Turning

87

to Rachel, he asked, "Think you can make us some popcorn?" Soon everyone was seated.

It was very relaxing and restful for Lisa. The birds were singing and it was just nice not to be working all the time.

"I suppose this is very different from your home," Jeff commented casually. "I guess it would take some adjusting to live on a farm. I know it would take a while for me to adjust to living in a city!"

Lisa wasn't sure how to answer. "Oh, I don't know," she replied. "We don't have cows, if that's what you mean. But the city is pretty in its own special way. Of course, the town we live in isn't very big. We have lots of trees and grass."

"I know we've been very busy since you've been here, and I'm sorry for that. It's not always this busy here. It's just that this is a busy time of year," Mom interjected.

"I'm sure you all must find plenty of time to have fun, too," Lisa said.

"Sure we do," Dad nodded. "We find time to go canoeing, bike riding, and other things. Of course, we also try to learn to have fun working. It has taken some of our children longer to realize that work can be fun, but I think we're making pretty good headway in that regard."

"Oh, I think that work is fun, too," Lisa returned quickly, looking at Jeff. "I'm not afraid to work hard." Then, thinking that Dad's comment was somehow addressed to her, she added, "I hope I've not complained."

"I haven't heard you say a single word of complaint," Dad responded truthfully.

# Jeff McLean: His Courtship

"You have done many things to help us," Mom said. "And we are most thankful for your help. It must be hard, coming into a strange house, and being put to work the way we have done to you."

Lisa blushed a little. "I'm glad to be here," she said. "Everyone has been so nice to me."

It was quiet for several minutes, as everyone seemed to be searching for a good topic. Finally, Lisa asked, "Jeff, when you start farming, where will the men who work for you live? On the farm? In . . . what are they called . . . bunkhouses?"

Jeff tried unsuccessfully to suppress a grin. "I doubt if I'll ever have any men working for me. My farm will be much too small for that."

"Oh!" Lisa exclaimed significantly. "I guess I just thought you would hire some men to do the hard work, and you would be the boss." After a pause she added, "Are there any other jobs you've thought about?"

"No, not really," Jeff replied. "I've wanted to farm as long as I can remember. I really enjoy the work, and being outdoors in the changing seasons."

The conversation then moved to what other activities were going to take place at the McLean farm over the next several months. Lisa seemed amazed at all of the tasks awaiting the men, and even more amazed that they didn't seem overwhelmed by it all.

Again, it became silent. Jeff, thinking of a question that Mr. Harris had asked him, turned to Lisa and asked, "What are your dreams, Lisa? I mean, what do you hope for the future?"

Lisa hesitated a little. "I hope to someday be married to the man God has chosen for me. I would

# Jeff McLean: His Courtship

like a few children . . . some boys like cute little Samuel over there would be great!" She thought some more. "I would also like to continue doing volunteer work. That is so rewarding to me. Maybe even be some kind of a leader in a volunteer organization, I don't know. Oh, and I would like to have a salt water tank for tropical fish someday," she added a little lightly. "Do you like fish, Jeff?"

Jeff laughed, "Just ask Mom. I eat two or three huge pieces every time she serves fish!" Then, being more serious, he added, "Little fish in tanks to look at are pretty. I enjoy watching them swim around."

Conversations continued for a while longer, until Dad stood up and announced, "It's time for me to head to bed. I've got work to do tomorrow." Before long, everyone went to bed.

The next afternoon, Dad suggested that everyone go over and see how Jeff's farm was progressing. Although he hadn't been able to work on it for several weeks, there were changes that some family members hadn't seen. Also, it was a chance for Lisa to see Jeff's place.

As they pulled into the driveway, Mom was watching Lisa's reaction. Lisa was very aware of this and tried her best to be cheerful and very impressed. "Oh, do you own *all* of this?" she said happily. "There are *so* many buildings!"

"Yes, there are many buildings," Jeff agreed. "Many that need fixing up, at that."

As the group walked the grounds and visited the buildings, it was harder for Lisa to show excitement. Everything looked so abandoned. It looked like someone hadn't lived there for years and years. She

# Jeff McLean: His Courtship

saw a mouse in the basement and screamed.

"That's okay," Mom assured her. "I scream too sometimes, when a mouse suddenly appears."

Lisa felt better from Mom's words. Yet, would she feel good about living here every day? Of that she wasn't at all sure. "Will there be mice when you're through fixing it all up?" she asked Jeff.

"I suppose there will always be an occasional mouse, although I'll seal up everything as well as I can. Mice just find ways to get into farm houses."

Lisa shivered at the thought of having to come down into this basement to do her laundry. In fact, she didn't even want to be down there any longer right now. "Can we go outside and see what the outside looks like?" she suggested.

Everyone moved to the front yard. Many of the flowers were up and there was pretty color everywhere. Lisa didn't seem to even notice. She just keep looking at the house with a rather worried look on her face.

"It does need a lot of work," Jeff said, trying to help her see beyond the mess of today. "But I think it can be a beautiful place, once all of the work is done."

Lisa didn't say anything. After a while, the group returned to the McLean farm.

# Chapter Eleven

With her rest, Janet was improving daily, just as the doctor had hoped she would.  Lisa continued doing whatever jobs Mom asked her to do.  She washed clothes, washed dishes, scrubbed floors, planted more seeds in the garden, and even helped do some mending.

To be honest, Lisa was getting tired of all of this work, and it was beginning to show.  Where she had once tried to hide her dislike for some of the work, she no longer tried as much.  So far, Jeff had not seemed terribly interested in her.  Of course, she wasn't quite sure how much he was supposed to show his interest in her, until a formal courtship was agreed upon.  Still, she started wishing she were back home, where life was much easier.  Lisa began to have a pouty countenance as she went about her tasks.  She still did the work, but no longer attempted to appear cheerful.  *Jeff doesn't seem to be noticing anyway*, she thought.

But Jeff had noticed.  And now he certainly noticed the change in Lisa's attitude.

On Tuesday of the second week of Lisa's visit, Mom had asked her if she would like to prepare the pumpkin custard for supper.  "Here's the directions on how to do it," Mom said, smiling at Lisa.  "I wrote it all out so you shouldn't have any trouble."  With that, Mom left the room to check on Janet.

Upon returning to the kitchen, she noticed that Lisa was putting a fourth egg yolk into the mixture.  "Lisa, I believe the recipe only calls for two egg yolks."

"I know, but we use six at our house," Lisa said. "It makes the custard much richer." She broke another egg into the bowl. "A really good cook uses lots of eggs," she finished with emphasis.

Rachel was standing in the kitchen as this exchange took place. She couldn't believe what Lisa had just done. Mom was used to her daughters following her directions. This was a serious violation of respect in her eyes.

It was in Jeff's eyes also. He was just entering the kitchen to get a drink of water as it occurred. Jeff was angry. It wasn't just the fact that Lisa had not respected Mom's wishes about the custard. It was the way in which she looked at Mom. She had a defiant look on her face as she spoke to Mom. Jeff moved toward the sink to get his water.

"Oh hi, Jeff," Lisa greeted, seeing Jeff for the first time. "Here, let me get some water for you. You look hot and tired."

"I'll get it myself," Jeff replied brusquely. "I know how to get water."

Dad had been right behind Jeff and heard this exchange. After getting a drink of water for himself, Dad followed Jeff back outside. "Come here, Jeff," Dad said. "You were a little rude, don't you think?"

"Maybe so, Dad," Jeff admitted, not cooling down much. He was still angry that Lisa had acted toward Mom as she had. "Look, I don't think this courtship is going to work out. And besides, she was rude to Mom. She's going to be leaving in a few days, and then we can move on with our lives."

Dad was surprised at that. He hadn't known that

# Jeff McLean: His Courtship

Jeff had decided that Lisa was not going to be someone he would court. However, that didn't excuse his behavior. "Look, son, whether you court her or not, makes no difference. You are not to be rude."

"Maybe you weren't in there yet, and didn't see the way she talked to Mom," Jeff countered, defensively.

"It makes no difference!" Dad replied. "Do two wrongs make a right? Of course not. If she was rude, that still gives you no license to be rude to her. Can't you see how wrong you are?"

Jeff kicked a rock and looked off toward the barn. He had to admit to himself that he had let his emotions get carried away. After a few moments of silence, he acknowledged, "I'm sorry, Dad. Yes, I guess I was wrong."

"It's not me you have to apologize to," Dad said sternly. "She's in the house."

Jeff summoned his courage and returned to the kitchen. He walked slowly over toward where Lisa was working. "I . . . I'm sorry," he stumbled. "I shouldn't have been rude to you a few minutes ago. Will you forgive me?"

Lisa was impressed with Jeff's humbleness. "You weren't rude," she replied.

"Yes, I was and I'm sorry," Jeff repeated.

"I forgive you, but I still don't think you were rude," Lisa said.

"Thank you," Jeff answered, and slowly walked out of the kitchen.

In a few days, the Harrises came to pick Lisa up. Although Mr. and Mrs. Harris were cordial and obviously enjoyed the company of Dad and Mom, anyone could see that they were sad about something.

"I was saddened when Lisa called us the other night and told us she wasn't interested in pursuing a courtship with Jeff," Mr. Harris said to Dad. "I'm sorry that it's not going to work out. We were hoping that this was God's provision for a godly husband for Lisa. Apparently she doesn't feel that being a farmer's wife is something she wants to consider."

"I understand. It's not for everyone," Dad replied. "Jeff didn't feel it was going to work either." He was sorry for Mr. Harris' sake. However, in talking with Jeff, he felt the Lord had led Jeff to make his decision.

After supper, the Harrises gathered at the door to leave. "Thank you so much for your help, Lisa," Mom said. "We can never thank you enough. Not only for all the help you gave us, but also for the way you cheered Janet up."

Lisa smiled. "I'm glad I could come and help." Then turning to Janet she added, "Remember, it's your turn to write me next! Goodbye everyone!"

As the car drove out of the driveway, Jeff spoke to his dad. "Dad, I think it would be helpful to go over again what to look for in a godly woman. Although I've studied the Scriptures and you've talked about it many times, could you maybe discuss it again with me?" Jeff asked. "I'm counting on you and Mom to help me in this decision process. Yet, I need to have more discernment myself. And I need to have those traits that are important clearly in my mind."

Dad thought for a minute. "Why don't I do this? Let me study it some more myself and put some thoughts together. Then I'll share my teaching with

# Jeff McLean: His Courtship

the whole family. How does that sound? It's something that everyone needs to hear."

"That's great," Jeff agreed. "The girls need to know what they should become and it's never too soon for Ben and Steve to learn what to look for either."

# Chapter Twelve

B ible time!" Ben called up the stairs a few weeks later. "It's time for Bible. Come on down, Samuel and Steve."

When everyone was seated, Dad led the family in several verses they were memorizing. Then he reached for his Bible and began. "I have been studying about the traits of a godly wife."

Everyone looked at Jeff.

"Yes, I'm sure Jeff wants to hear about them. But I want to share them with all of you, because they really do apply to you all," Dad continued. "Ben and Steve, and yes, even you Samuel, will need to know these as you look for a wife. I know that will be a long time away, yet it doesn't hurt to start recognizing the traits of a godly woman now."

"I want to marry Becky," Samuel stated plainly.

"Well, in time God will reveal to you the woman you are to marry," Dad smiled. "For now, just listen and learn, okay little man?"

Dad turned to the girls. "You girls also need to reflect on these things. Examine your own lives to see if you are living up to the principles and character traits I'll discuss. If not, ask God to help you, through the power of the Holy Spirit, to change and be conformed to the image He has planned for your life."

"Me too," volunteered Mom. "I'm going to be listening, too."

"Good," Dad said. "Even I need to be aware of

these as I help each of you look for a godly wife or help you become one. So, let's begin."

Dad turned in his Bible and read Titus 2. "The Bible gives us lots of instruction about a godly woman. I'm going to go over some of the traits she should have, although there are obviously lots of others. Titus 2 is the passage we will look at tonight. The first trait listed is sober. Jeff, this is the same idea as we talked about for men. It means to be self controlled as to opinion or passion. It also is translated discreet or temperate. This can be especially hard for women, who tend to be more emotional than men. But even though God made many women more emotional, He still expects them to be in control of those emotions. They shouldn't hide behind the phrase 'I'm just emotional' to justify being out of control. A woman also needs to know how to control the expression of her opinion. There will be many times in a marriage where it will be best for a wife *not* to express her opinion, especially if the couple is following the Biblical model of the wife being in submission to her husband."

"How could you see if a woman was sober, Dad?" asked Jeff. "I mean, before marriage, when you are just going through a courtship with her?"

"That's an excellent question," Dad praised. "In fact, that question can be asked of most of the traits we will cover. First, I think it's important to ask the Holy Spirit to give you special discernment in discovering these things. He can reveal them to you. Also, I think it is important to talk to the young lady about these topics and see what she says about them. Of course, she may just tell you what she thinks you want to hear."

"We can all be guilty of that," Jeff offered.

"So true," Dad agreed. "Don't overlook the discernment that your parents can provide in looking for these traits. After all, one benefit of having parents involved in the courtship is to provide such counsel. And when it comes to evaluating young women, listen carefully to what your mother says. She's a woman, too, and can often have special insight into what a young woman is thinking and whether she has these traits.

"With regard to soberness specifically," Dad said, getting back to Jeff's original question, "I would want to see if the young woman is frequently trying to make sure her opinions or thoughts are the most important. Of course, if she were in a confrontation with someone with different opinions, you could more easily see how self-controlled she is.

"The second trait mentioned in Titus 2 is that a godly woman should love her husband. The Greek word there means 'affectionate as a wife' and comes from a root word which means friendly. Basically, the idea is that the wife should be friendly toward her husband."

"Isn't that rather obvious?" Janet asked. "I mean, wouldn't all wives be friendly toward their husbands?"

"You would think so," Dad agreed. "The reality, however, is that many couples aren't friends at all. In my opinion, the husband and wife should not just be friends, they should be each other's best friend. They should want to spend time with each other, rather than try to find other people to spend their time with."

"That's going to be a hard one to observe," Jeff

commented.

"Yes, it will be," Dad nodded.  "You can try to assess if the young woman is friendly toward you and whether you think that friendship might grow.  In everyday life, not even thinking of courtship right now, as you meet new people you tend to have a sense of whether they might turn out to be friends or just acquaintances.  Also, I would want to see how many 'outside activities' she is engaged in now and see if she intends to keep involved in them all after marriage."

Dad looked at some notes he had prepared for this teaching.  "Let's see.  A godly woman should also love her children.  That means to be fond of her children, friendly toward them, in a maternal sense.  I know that the woman you may court doesn't have any children.  And yet, is there evidence that she loves children in general?  Has she availed herself of opportunities to be around and help with children?  When?  For what purpose?  Was it just to make money babysitting?  As you ask these questions, be aware that there are many different personalities out there.  Some people are naturally outgoing; they are called extroverts.  Others tend to be less outgoing, and keep things within themselves; these are called introverts.  Don't make a mistake and think that just because someone is an introvert that they somehow don't like children.  Again, you will have to rely heavily on the Holy Spirit for discernment.

"In verse five of Titus 2, the trait of 'discreet' is mentioned. Since this means essentially the same thing as soberness, which was mentioned in verse four, some might ask, 'Why mention the same thing twice?' I can't answer that question.  The Bible doesn't tell us.

# Jeff McLean: His Courtship

Maybe it was because the writer knew that women might have trouble with this trait. Maybe it was mentioned because it is very important. I just don't know.

"Moving on, verse five instructs godly women to be chaste. That means clean in a figurative sense, as opposed to literally keeping their bodies clean from dirt and grime. The Greek word means innocent, modest, and perfect and is translated chaste, clean, and pure in the Bible. While it has many applications, an important one is sexual purity. It is important for a godly woman to keep herself pure, not only in her behavior but even in her thoughts. It is also important for a woman to help the men she comes in contact with to stay pure. Although the men are responsible before God for their thoughts and actions, a woman shouldn't do things which would encourage their behavior or thoughts to be displeasing to God. We'll talk about this some more, but for now I'll just mention that this includes things like how a woman dresses, the makeup she uses, her posture, her expressions, and what she says."

"Some women don't wear modest clothes," Becky said. "I point them out to Mom when we're shopping."

"That's true," Dad said. "It's easy sometimes to spot someone who is maybe even attempting to be immodest on purpose. That's sad. What we also want to avoid, however, is being immodest even though we're not trying to be. You girls can always ask Mom or me our opinion about your clothing."

Dad looked at his list again. "The next trait is one that really ruffles some feathers today. The Bible says that a godly woman should be a keeper at home. That means a stayer at home, someone who is domestically inclined. A woman should desire to be at home, not long to be somewhere else. The word 'housekeeper' is not in vogue today, neither is 'housewife.' Yet, until recently that is what most women in our country would categorize themselves as being. It is sad that our culture has denigrated those terms to be shameful in many women's eyes. God is pleased when a woman is a keeper at home. How can you spot a woman with this trait?" Dad asked, anticipating Jeff's question. "I suppose you can look at her life now, before she is married. Where does she spend her time and focus her thoughts right now? On domestic things? Or on things that tend to take her out of her home? I think this is one of those areas where the Holy Spirit is going to have to provide discernment."

"Dad, should we never go to the grocery store?" Rachel asked. "That's not being a keeper at home."

Dad smiled. "Being a keeper at home doesn't imply that you never leave the house, Rachel. It does mean that a woman desires to be at home and be involved in the tasks that she has been given by God to perform. For most married women, that includes raising and nurturing her children at home.

"A godly woman should be good, according to verse five. That is a general term that sums up all of what a Christian life should be like. The dictionary says that the word is a general term of approval or commendation. I think of it as a noticeable trait that reflects the right heart inside the woman. The opposite would be someone who does not elicit approval because their hearts, minds, and actions are not pleasing to God. You can think of it as a global assessment or as item-specific."

Dad laughed at the look of bewilderment on Steve's face. "That just means that you can refer to a woman as good when you take into account all of her traits; that would be a global assessment. Or, you can be item-specific, like saying that she would be good with children or that she is good at being sober.

"The final trait I'll discuss tonight is that a godly woman should be obedient to her husband. It is mentioned here in Titus 2, but is also clearly taught in Ephesians 5:22-24, Colossians 3:18, and in I Peter 3:1, 5-6. I looked up the Greek word for obedient, and it means the following: to be under obedience to, to put under, to subdue unto, to be subject to, and to submit self unto. Anyway you look at it, you still come to the same conclusion. God has ordained a hierarchal structure in the family. In fact, I Corinthians 11:3 states that the head of the woman is man. The father is the leader and head and the wife is to be in submission to his leadership. This does **not** mean, however, that the wife is to sin if her husband tells her to do something that is sinful. God never wants us to sin!

The wife being in submission to the husband is totally opposite to what the world would have you to believe, yet that is what God's Holy Word teaches again and again. In fact, the Bible says here in Titus 2 that if a wife isn't obedient, and perhaps isn't the other things we have been discussing tonight, that the word of God is blasphemed. That's strong!"

"How can you know if a woman would be obedient to her husband, before she gets married?" Ben asked. It was encouraging that Dad had everyone's attention.

"Well, even before she is married, a woman is to be in submission.  First, she is to be in submission to God.  How is she doing in that area?  Is she obeying God's commands for her life, or does she find excuses not to obey and submit to His will?  Second, she is to be submissive to her parents.  How is she doing in that regard?  Does she try to second-guess them all the time or try to make her own decisions?  I also think that this is an area that a man and woman should talk about as they go through a courtship.  Of course, remember that words are easier than actions.  But you can at least find out what her words and thoughts are on this subject.  Has she followed the wrong advice and teaching of the world?  Or has she remained pure to the Word of God?"

"But Dad, many girls haven't been taught this principle," Rachel offered.  "I don't think it is something that many churches talk about."

Dad looked a little sad.  "You're right, Rachel. I'm afraid that many pastors in our churches are following the teachings of the world, rather than those of God.  But, even if a woman has never heard good teaching on this subject, is she open to it?  Is she willing, by the power of the Holy Spirit, to be in submission to her husband?  That is what I would want to find out before I married someone."

"But you're already married," Samuel said. "Mom's your wife, Dad!"

Everyone laughed.  "That's right, Samuel.  Mom is my wife.  And a good wife she is too!  I was just talking as though I were someone going through courtship, that's all.  Sorry if I've confused you.

# Jeff McLean: His Courtship

"The Bible has so much more to say about what a godly woman is like," Dad concluded. "But I'll save that for another time. Let's pray and ask God to make us the man or woman that He wants us to be. Not the man or woman that the world wants us to be." With that, the family knelt for a time of prayer and dedication to do the will of God.

# Chapter Thirteen

That next evening, after supper, Dad called everyone into the living room.  "Let's have our Bible and prayer time now."  When everyone was seated, he began.  "You will recall that I was discussing the traits of a godly woman yesterday.  I want to finish discussing those traits tonight.  Are you all ready?"  After going over their memory verses, Dad started teaching.

"As I mentioned last night, there are many traits that a godly woman should possess.  First of all, she should follow all of the commands and desires of God which are recorded in Scripture.  We are going to continue to focus, however, on those characteristics which are specifically mentioned about women or wives.  Let's look first at the familiar passage found in Proverbs 31:10-31.

"In verses eleven and twelve, the Bible says the husband of a godly wife 'doth safely trust in her' and that she won't do him evil.  The Hebrew word there for 'trust' means 'to be confident or sure.'  What is this referring to?  What can the husband trust his wife for?  What can he be confident or sure about?"  Everyone in the room was silent.

"Let's look at the context of those verses.  Right after verse twelve, the Bible lists many activities that the godly woman will be involved in, including making clothing, and securing food and preparing it in a timely manner.  It also mentions securing merchandise, presumably the things that her household needs in order to function properly.  From that context, I

# Jeff McLean: His Courtship

believe verse eleven means that the husband can trust his wife to faithfully perform her domestic duties. Now, how could you spot those traits in a young woman before marriage? I would want to know if she has domestic skills already and the extent to which she is developing those skills. I would also want to talk to her parents and find out if her parents can count on her to perform the duties that she has been assigned, in a timely manner. If they give her a task to do, like make supper or clean a room, can they count on her to get it done on time without having to remind her?"

"You mean that some man will ask that about me someday?" asked Becky, soberly. Just this morning Mom had reprimanded Becky several times for fooling around instead of doing the dishes.

"Yes, I wouldn't be surprised if a young man did ask me that," Dad answered, smiling at his youngest daughter. "Of course, that *probably* won't happen in the next six months for you." Everyone laughed. "Yet, it's never too early to develop those skills. You see, if you're not caring enough to do your jobs well now, why will you change when you get married?"

Dad paused a moment to let that lesson sink in, then he continued looking at Proverbs 31. "Verses thirteen through twenty-seven talk about a lot of jobs that the godly woman is involved in. It is obvious that she works hard at home. She gets up early, stays up late, and has a solid work ethic. That is summarized in verse twenty-seven where it says she 'eateth not the bread of idleness.' To be idle means not inclined to work or lazy. Well, a godly woman is not lazy when it comes to doing her jobs around the house. If I were examining a young woman with an eye toward possibly marrying her, I would want to know that she was not lazy. Does she have the trait of working hard? I would want to watch what she does at her parents' home. I would also hope to learn that she has been trained for this trait from her early years, by being assigned meaningful chores."

"We do chores," Samuel offered.

"Yes, you do," Dad agreed. Then he looked back at his notes. "Verse twenty says that a godly woman helps the needy and poor. In fact, this trait is commanded of all Christians and is discussed in many places in the Bible, including Deuteronomy 15:11, Proverbs 22:9, Romans 12:13, and Ephesians 4:28. I would want to see if the young woman had a helping, compassionate spirit."

"How would you know that?" Janet asked. "She could claim to have compassion and yet just be pretending."

"That's right," Dad nodded. "In fact, that's true of most things we are talking about. It's one thing to claim you have something, but quite another matter to actually put your talk into action. So, I would also look for behaviors that demonstrate compassion toward the poor. Perhaps she might, in the course of your courtship, spontaneously call your attention to someone in need.

"Verse thirty says that a godly woman 'feareth the Lord.' The word 'feareth' in that verse means reverent, or afraid. Does the young woman fear the Lord? Does she realize the majesty of God Almighty? Or is she, at times, flippant or irreverent as she talks about God? Pray that we would all be careful in this regard. I'm afraid that many people spend so much time

# Jeff McLean: His Courtship

talking about God being our friend, that they tend to think of Him as they would their next door neighbor. He is not. He is the God of the universe, Creator of all things, Who knows all things, sees all things, and Who has always existed.

"Let's look up a few more verses." Looking at his notes, he continued, "Turn with me to I Timothy 2:9-15." After reading the verses, Dad said, "Modest apparel. That is something we touched on last night. In this passage, several more directions are given as guidance. A woman should adorn herself with shame-facedness. I know what some of you are wondering; what does shamefacedness mean? Well, in this context it refers to bashfulness toward men, having downcast eyes. Again, that is very different from what the world will teach you. The world would like to see women be bold toward men. The verses also mention sobriety again. Self control is always important in a godly woman's life. The Bible then talks about a woman's apparel. It is clear that your apparel, including your hair, clothing, and jewelry, should not attract attention to yourself. I Peter 3:3-4 echoes the same thoughts and goes on to say that, instead, a woman should have a meek and quiet spirit. If I were evaluating a young woman for possible courtship, I would ask myself how she is doing in this area. Is it her apparel that is attracting you to her? Or is it her quiet and meek spirit that is attracting you to her? Those are serious questions and require serious and honest answers.

"Reading further in the verses, we find that a woman is to learn in silence. She is not to teach men or have authority over men. In a related vein, I

Corinthians 14:34 instructs women to be silent in the churches. I would want to see what kind of teaching a young woman has received about these verses. I would want to talk to her about them as well as observe her actual behavior. For example, is the young woman I am courting trying to teach me even as we court?"

"But what if the husband is confused about something and has it all wrong?" Rachel asked. "What if they don't really understand what the Bible is saying in some verse? Shouldn't the wife teach her husband the truth in that situation if she really does understand the verse?"

"I don't think so," Dad answered gently. "I know that others will disagree with me. But when I study scripture I find that God has set up a system for leadership and teaching that He developed. We need to follow it. I believe that when we follow the Bible's plan that God will bless much more than if a wife takes matters into her own hands and tries to teach her husband.

"The next set of verses I want to examine are found in I Timothy 5:11-13. These are written specifically for young widows, and it may be that young widows potentially have more of a problem with the things mentioned here. But I believe they have direct application for all women. The Bible instructs women not to be idle, wandering from house to house, being busybodies and tattlers. There are several applications here to look for in a potential mate. Is the young woman a gossip? Does she prefer to spend most of her time visiting with her friends instead of staying at home tending to domestic duties? Does she tend to read books in which the main characters do these kinds of things all day long?  I would be concerned if the answer to any of these questions is 'yes.'

"There are many traits that a godly woman should have.  Let's look at one more.  A godly woman should not be contentious.  That means one who is always ready to argue, a woman who is quarrelsome and belligerent.  Proverbs 19:13 says that the contentions of a wife are a continual dropping.  It is an unending irritation, like a faucet that drips in the night and won't let you sleep.  Proverbs 21:9 says that it is better to live on one corner of the roof than with a brawling woman in a comfortable house."

"That's funny," Steve said.  "I can just see a husband sitting up on his roof while his wife is hanging out the window, shouting up to him, still trying to argue with him about something."

"It may seem funny, but it's no fun," Dad commented.  "Proverbs 21:19 says that it would be better to live in a wilderness than with a contentious and angry woman.  You want to escape from such a woman.  Climb up on your roof, run to the desert, anywhere to get away from such a woman."

"Is anyone really like that?" asked Steve seriously.

"Yes, I'm afraid that some women are like that," Dad replied.  "I have known a number of men who give in on things that they don't think are wise or in which they don't believe just to avoid incurring their wives' quarrelsome spirits.  I've known men who moved to a new house, men who let their children do things that they didn't believe were best, and men who have bought thousands of dollars worth of furniture, cars, and other things against their better judgement, just to avoid arguing with their wives.  In fact, it's one reason that some men stay late at work or stop at a bar on the way home.  No one wants to be near a contentious woman."

"That's serious," Jeff reflected.  "Mom doesn't have a problem with that, so I'm not sure I would be able to notice it in a young woman.  How can you spot it, Dad?"

"If a young woman has a really serious problem with it, believe me, you'll be able to see it easily enough.   In order to spot it in those who just have a tendency to be contentious there are perhaps several things I would look for.  Does she have to have *her* way, or else?  In other words, will she not give up on something until she wins?   One indicator would be if she has a 'correcting spirit'."

"What's that?" questioned Ben.   "I thought a godly woman would be able to correct her children when they do something wrong."

"She should correct and discipline her children; that's not what I meant when I said a correcting spirit," Dad explained.  "I'm referring to a tendency to correct people they are talking to on minor points. Let's say I am telling a story about Jeff's childhood, and as a minor point, I casually mention that he was eleven when we got our first dog.  Mom knows that Jeff was actually twelve when we got our dog.  That's not an important point, and she probably shouldn't bring my mistake to my attention.  Someone who has the problem of a 'correcting spirit' would interrupt me and tell me that in fact, Jeff was twelve years old when it happened.  Someone with that problem would tend to do that kind of thing a lot."

# Jeff McLean: His Courtship

"I know someone with a correcting spirit," Steve offered quickly. He was about to reveal the identity of the person when Dad interrupted him.

"We don't need to list those we know who have this problem," Dad said. "We need to make sure we don't have a problem with it. If we do, we need to ask God to help us change."

Dad folded his notes. "That's a lot for one evening. Let's stop there and have a time of prayer. Let's pray that God would be working in the lives of the young women who might go through a courtship with our boys, that they would strive to have the character traits we have mentioned tonight. It would also be good for the women in our house to ask God to help them do the same thing." After prayer, the family stood and started walking out of the living room.

"Mommy," Samuel confided, grabbing Mom's hand and looking up into her eyes, "you must be a godly woman. You don't do the bad stuff that Dad talked about."

"Thank you for saying so, Samuel," Mom replied, scooping him up and giving him a big hug. "Will you please remember to pray for me that I would always do God's will?"

Samuel thought about that for a moment as though he wasn't sure if he would or not. Finally, he answered, "Yes, I *will* pray for you, Mommy." Mom gave him another hug and carried him up the stairs.

After the little ones were in bed and things had settled down a bit, Dad and Jeff went to the porch to sit. Jeff spoke first. "That was some helpful teaching,

# Jeff McLean: His Courtship

Dad. Thanks. I think I have a better feel for what to look for now."

"Just ask God for discernment and guidance, and keep His Word open, and you should be okay," Dad replied. "Also, remember that a woman will continue to mature in Christ after she is married. Is there anything you learned from the situation with Lisa that can help you as you move forward in your search?"

Jeff thought for a few minutes. "I definitely need to seek your and Mom's counsel more often. At first, I didn't really see anything wrong with her at all."

"We did notice some things that concerned us. We weren't hiding them from you, though. We didn't want to make any rash assessments and were trying to give her the benefit of the doubt. After all, she was in a stressful situation, since she wasn't in her own house, and was having to do work for people who were almost total strangers. In fact, I was planning on talking to you about some of them on the day that you told me you weren't interested in pursuing the possibility with Lisa any longer."

"She was a very nice young lady in many ways," Jeff observed. "That's one thing that makes it all so hard."

"Yes, she was a very nice young lady," Dad agreed. "I trust that she will continue to mature as a Christian. I think she will make someone a wonderful wife someday, if she allows the Holy Spirit to continue to sanctify her. Did you learn anything else?"

"Well, I guess I learned, at least in a situation like this, to be pretty careful about someone you've never met in person. I mean, someone can sound really wonderful on the phone or in letters, like Lisa did.

# Jeff McLean:  His Courtship

However, when you get the chance to observe some-one for a long time, the real person shines through," Jeff reflected.  "I'm not saying that Lisa was awful or anything, Dad," he added.

"I know you're not, son."

"I also think I've learned the importance of being honest with myself," Jeff acknowledged.

"What do you mean?" asked Dad.

Jeff struggled to put his thoughts into words. "How can I say this?  I guess I saw some things early on that concerned me about Lisa.  Yet, I wanted to push them out of my mind and only focus on the positive things I saw.  I never want to just focus on the negative things about anyone, because none of us are perfect.  And yet, I need to be able to not just forget about them either.  It's a fine line, I guess.  Anyway, what I'm saying is that I need to seriously look for and remember *all* the traits that are displayed, good and bad.  Only then can I start to accurately summarize what someone is like."

"That's true," Dad said.  "I think all of us tend to want to push negative things out of our minds. Especially about someone that we are even remotely considering marrying.  Yet, the time to examine those traits in a logical, objective sense is before marriage. I think you're wise to see the importance of doing that."

"I also want to remember to be myself in a situa-tion like I was in for those couple of weeks," Jeff admitted.  "I'm afraid I sort of found myself trying to be a little better than I actually am sometimes.  I wasn't exactly trying to impress Lisa, but it doesn't seem fair for me to pretend to be someone that I'm not."

"What do you mean?" questioned Mom, who had joined the pair on the porch.

Jeff tried to think of a good example. "Well, when she would talk about living in town and how she liked to shop in some of those fancy stores, I kind of acted like I would like to do that too. And you both know that nothing could be further from the truth! The only stores I really like are feed stores and farm implement stores. I never actually said I would like to go in those fancy stores, but I think I still tried to give her that impression. That was misleading on my part."

"I'm with you about shopping, Jeff," laughed Dad. "I think most people are going to naturally try to put their best foot forward when they are courting someone. Yet, we are to be truthful and not deceitful in any way. You would be wise to be yourself so that the other person can really get to know who they might someday marry."

"I don't know what you two have said so far," Mom interjected. "But I'd like to apologize, Jeff, for not coming to you sooner with some of the things I learned about Lisa. I suppose I kept thinking to myself how much I liked her mother, and how nice it would be to be related to them. At first, I wanted to only report the good things. I would have told you soon, though."

"That's okay, Mom," Jeff said. "We've all learned from the process."

Jeff noticed that it was getting late. Looking at his Mom and Dad, he smiled and suggested, "I would like to pray with you both now, if that's okay." Jeff bowed his head and prayed, "Dear Lord, we thank you for the lessons you are teaching us. Forgive us for the many times and the many ways in which we have failed You. Please give us direction as we seek Your mate for my life. Help me to mature as a man of God. And please be with Lisa. Help her to grow in Christ, and I pray that you would help her to find the mate You have chosen for her, if that is Your will. Thank you for loving us. In Jesus Name, amen."

# Chapter Fourteen

As the months passed, Jeff worked on his farm. He plowed, disced, and harrowed his hay fields, then replanted them in clover and alfalfa. While he was doing this, he also finished the drainage work that was needed. "Now that's a pretty field," Dad commented, looking over one field that Jeff had just finished. "Hopefully next year we can cut some hay off of it."

"I hope so," Jeff commented. "It would be nice to get something off the farm, instead of just pumping things into it constantly." Of course, the biggest "thing" that Jeff was pumping into his farm was his own labor.

Another top priority on Jeff's list was to fix the pasture fences. Because the fencing was so old, Jeff decided to replace all of the old fence posts with new cedar ones. "It's a tradeoff," Jeff told a friend who questioned the wisdom of spending so much time and effort. "I could put cheaper posts in, but then I'd just have to replace them in ten years or so." It was obvious that Jeff intended to live at this farm for a long time.

Putting a new roof on the house, which Jeff did a year later,  proved to be more work than Jeff originally anticipated.  Since there were already several layers of old shingles, it was best to remove them all before putting on the new ones. As he removed the last layer of shingles, he found a number of rotten boards that needed replacing. When he pried away some of those rotten boards, he found a few roof joists that had also rotted.

"Well, at least when I'm through with all this," he said, sighing to his dad who was helping, "I shouldn't have to worry about the roof for a long time.  I had no idea there was so much damage."

After replacing the roof joists and the rotten roof pieces, he rolled on new tar paper and began shingling. As anyone can tell you who has done it, it's hard, hot work.  The dark tar paper absorbed the summer heat and radiated it to the sweating men who were standing on top of it.  Still, it was a pleasure, when they took much-needed breaks in the shade of some trees, to look up and see the new, straight shingles they had just installed.  The roofing was also made difficult by the many dormers and different slopes where the various roof sections met.  It took the two men over three weeks, working as they found time, to get the new roof completed.

"Isn't it beautiful, Mom?" Jeff asked, when his mom came to inspect the results of the men's hard work.

"It certainly is," Mom agreed, hugging Jeff. "You're going to have a nice house here.  I'm thankful you are able to work on it like this and save yourself so much money."

"God has blessed me, there's no doubt about that," Jeff agreed.  Thankfully, he had been able to make a few larger payments on the remaining balance of the farm, due to some good years of calving and the price of beef going up.  It looked like he would have the farm paid off earlier than he expected, God willing.

So, the years went by.  Jeff celebrated his twenty-fourth and twenty-fifth birthdays.  Most everyone who

# Jeff McLean:  His Courtship

knew him would have agreed that Jeff was blessed.
Things seemed to be working out for him so well.

Yet, there was still a void in his life.  No one new
had moved into their area that was committed to
courtship. Although Jeff tried not to be disappointed,
he did have days and weeks in which he doubted if he
would ever find someone to be his mate for life.
"What am I doing wrong?" he asked his dad.  "It
seems like everything is going well for me.  Yet, it
doesn't look like there is anyone for me to marry.  Do
you think I'm doing anything wrong?"

Dad thought for a moment.  "Your mom and I
have talked about this," Dad admitted.  "No, I certainly don't think you're doing anything wrong.  It's
just that God hasn't shown  you anyone yet, that's
all." After pausing, Dad said, "You know, God never
promised that he would bring a wife into your life.
And he never promised that he would bring a wife to
you right away.  I know those aren't encouraging
words, and not ones that you want to hear, but they
need to be said."

Both men were silent for a long time thinking
about the implications of what Dad had just said.  If
God wasn't going to bring a wife into Jeff's life for
several years, he knew he could handle that.  *But what
if God never wants me to get married?* Jeff thought.
*I'm not sure what I would do then.*

Dad must have read Jeff's thoughts from his facial
expressions.  "Jeff, remember that whatever God
chooses to do in your life, He has promised that He
would never leave you nor forsake you.  Whatever He
has planned for you, will be His plan, and so it will be
perfect in every way.  I guess what I'm saying is that

# Jeff McLean: His Courtship

God will supply your needs and help you to find comfort and contentment in whatever He brings to you."

Jeff knew that. He had studied the Scriptures for years and was well aware of the promises they contained. Somehow it seemed easy for Dad to be saying that, since Dad already had a wife and children, and his dreams had come true. Still, there was truth in what Dad said. What more could Jeff do anyway?

Months passed. Months in which Jeff worked at both his dad's farm and on his own farm. By now the fields, pasture, and barn were in pretty good shape. The farm house had a new roof, but inside there was still a lot of work to be done. Jeff had done no painting or tidying up inside the farmhouse since Mrs. Walters moved out. He had spent most of his efforts where most farmers would: in the areas where the farm would actually earn him a living.

"Jeff, are you going to get married?" Becky asked him one morning as she was hanging out laundry. Jeff was working nearby on the hydraulics of his tractor.

"Well, I don't know," Jeff responded. "That's up to God. So far, I've not met anyone that I feel He is leading me to."

"How about Phyllis at church?" Rachel chimed in. She was helping Becky hang the laundry. It was a beautiful sunny June morning.

Jeff smiled at Rachel. "Don't you think she's a little young?"

Rachel didn't think so. "She's going to be fifteen next month."

"And I turned twenty-five a few months ago. I

# Jeff McLean: His Courtship

think she's a little young to consider."

"I know," Becky jumped in, excitedly. "Jenny Barker is old enough."

Again Jeff smiled. The girls just didn't seem to understand. "Jenny Barker is a very nice girl, but she isn't old enough either."

"How old do you think she is?" Becky asked, a little defensively.

Jeff shook his head. "I don't know," he said. Jenny and her family had been worshiping at their fellowship for many years. Jeff remembered when he first met her. She was much younger than him — in fact, she had been a little girl when he was in his teens. Thus, he had always categorized her as being a member of the younger group at church. "Maybe she's fifteen or sixteen."

Rachel laughed. "Jeff, where have you been? I know how old Jenny is because her sister is one of my friends. Jenny had a birthday just last week and Amy, that's my friend who's her sister, gave her a new set of mixing bowls for her hope chest."

"Well, how old is she?" Becky asked.

"She just turned twenty," Rachel said. "Isn't that old enough?"

Jeff didn't answer. He was trying to figure this all out. "She can't be twenty years old. She is a lot younger than me."

"You can ask Mom," Rachel offered. "But I know she's twenty. Isn't that old enough?"

Jeff still didn't answer. There had been a big difference between a sixteen-year-old Jeff and an eleven-year-old Jenny. But as the years go by, there isn't that big a difference between someone twenty-

# Jeff McLean:  His Courtship

five and someone twenty.

Wetness.  Was it raining?  Jeff looked down at his pant's leg.  There was hydraulic oil spilling from a hose that he had just uncoupled when Rachel had told Jenny's age.  Quickly, he sealed the hose and stopped the flow of oil.  *Can she really be that old?*  Jeff wondered.

Becky and Rachel giggled and moved on to finish hanging their laundry.

When Jeff went into the house for  a drink, he casually asked Mom, "Say, Mom.  The girls and I were talking about some of the people at the church.  How old would you say Jenny Barker is?"

Mom thought for a second, then answered, "Eighteen or nineteen, I'd say."  She kneaded the dough some more, then stopped and stared at the dough.  "Now hold on.  I believe I remember Ruth saying something about her birthday last Sunday at church. Let me think . . ."  Mom stared at the hoosier as she thought, yet her hands continued kneading the dough.  "She's twenty.  Yes, she just turned twenty last week."

Jeff changed the subject, then walked out of the house.  He had some thinking to do.  He had not spent a lot of time talking to Jenny over the years, but had talked to her when their families got together a few times.  She seemed like a nice girl although he hadn't really thought of her for some time.  When he first started thinking of courtship, he and Dad had talked about the different girls in their fellowship and Jenny's name had come up.  At seventeen, she had been too young, in Jeff's opinion, to even consider.  *I guess I must have just totally removed her from consideration*

# Jeff McLean: His Courtship

*back then*, he thought. But the more he turned it over in his mind, the more he realized that everyone does grow up. Even Jenny!

Jeff decided to start observing Jenny a little more. He also spent time praying, to see if God might be leading in this. Weeks went by.

At church, he noticed that Jenny always dressed modestly. When he happened to pass Jenny talking with some other young women, he sensed that she was quiet and gentle. She seemed very happy, yet in control of her emotions. Some of the other young women at church didn't seem to display as much control when they laughed or talked.

As the weeks passed, Jeff felt an attraction toward Jenny that he had never felt before. As he continued to pray about it, he felt that the Lord was moving him to think of courting her. When he was reasonably sure of this, he sought out Dad and had a conversation.

"I would like to explore the possibility of courting Jenny Barker," he surprised his dad, announcing it in the barn one morning. "I've prayed about it and feel that the Lord is telling me to move ahead with your permission."

Dad, who was adding fuel to his tractor, was a little taken aback. "Well, I'm glad God has provided you some more direction, son. Really glad."

"What do we do now?" Jeff asked.

Dad answered right away. "I think it would be good to spend more time with her family before you formally ask to court her. You need opportunity to observe her traits and just get to know her better." After a pause, he continued, "Jenny Barker. Well, that's really a fine young lady. I thought you wrote

124

her off a few years back."

Jeff seemed a little embarrassed.  "I guess I forgot that everyone grows up, Dad.  Besides, maybe God just wanted me to wait until now so that I could mature more, myself.  I don't know.  I can't explain it.  All I do know is that I think I am supposed to pursue the matter at this time."

"That's great!" Dad beamed.  "I've always been impressed with Jenny.  She claims to be committed to courtship, and she acts like it, too."  Dad pulled the dipstick out of the tractor and rubbed it on a rag before reinserting it to check the level.  "Yes, she seems to be a fine young lady.  We've known her family for . . . let's see . . . I guess about ten years now.  A fine Christian man.  That's what Jim Barker is.  Ruth is outstanding, too."  He cocked his head to one side in thought.  "I wonder what Jim would think about a farmer marrying his daughter?"

The following week, Dad invited the Barkers over for dinner on Friday.

As Friday afternoon rolled around, Jeff started getting nervous.  "What's wrong?" Dad asked.  "You act like you're going to meet someone for the first time.  Remember, this is the same young lady we've been talking about and praying about for a while now.  You've known her since she was a little girl.  Settle down!"

"I'm not afraid of her," Jeff responded.  "I guess it's really just excitement.  Excitement that things are moving again."

"Want to know the truth?" Dad confided.  "I'm excited, too."

The evening went well.  As soon as the Barkers

# Jeff McLean:  His Courtship

entered the house, Jeff was much more relaxed.  He enjoyed his conversations with Jenny and with members of her family.  He was as impressed with her as he had been at church.

Over the summer months, Jeff and his dad tried to create opportunities for the two families to spend more time together.  They went canoeing together, and later visited a nearby state park.  The Barkers, in turn, had the McLeans over for a hot dog roast.  These visits gave Jeff the opportunity to observe Jenny and how she interacted with her parents and brothers and sisters.  In all of these situations, Jeff found her to be kind and compassionate.  For example, during the canoe trip, Ricky, her four-year-old brother, accidently dropped his sandwich out of the canoe.  Jenny quickly gave her sandwich to him and tried to cheer Ricky up by talking about how the fish would probably be surprised when they tasted egg salad for the first time.  Jeff was also impressed several times with Jenny's quick and willing obedience to her parents' wishes.

Jeff spent much time praying about God's will for his life.  As the weeks went by, he felt ever more peace about it and a stronger sense that God was leading in that particular direction.  Late in the summer, Jeff announced to his dad that he was ready to see if Jenny would agree to go through a courtship with him.  Dad agreed to relate this to Mr. Barker.  "We'll just have to see what her parents say and then what Jenny, herself, says," Dad commented.  "Let's keep praying."

"Dad, the phone's for you," Janet called to Dad in the barn yard, a few days later.

"Hello," Dad greeted.  "Oh hi, Jim . . .  Yes, we're

# Jeff McLean: His Courtship

doing fine . . . Good . . . Good . . . That's great! . . . Yes, as soon as possible . . . No, I think it's fine that you called. He would want to know as soon as possible . . . I hope you have a safe trip this morning and that your meeting goes well . . . Okay, goodbye."

That night after supper, Jeff announced that he was going to court Jenny Barker. Everyone was happy. Janet said that she had suspected this was coming for some time.

"I told you she was old enough," Becky said.

"When will you start?" asked Ben.

"I guess you could say that we've already started," Jeff said, laughing. "Will you all pray for me?"

"Let's do that right now, shall we?" Dad suggested. Everyone knelt by their chairs in the kitchen. "Dear Father, we pray for Jeff and Jenny as they embark on this very important and exciting phase of their lives. Please help all of us to have Your wisdom and discernment. We ask that Your will be done. May we grow closer to the image of your Son, in whose Name we pray. Amen."

# Chapter Fifteen

How marvelous, how wonderful, and my song shall ever be . . . " Jeff sang as he showered. Tonight he had been invited to spend the evening at the Barkers' home and he was so happy he thought he would explode. Dressing quickly, he was out the door in no time.

As he drove to the Barker home, he felt a need to pray. Sure, he was happy that the courtship was formally begun and looked forward to learning more about Jenny tonight, but he needed to remember the importance of looking for the character traits that Dad had talked about. After praying, he listed them in his mind: sober, one who will love her children and husband, chaste, a keeper at home, obedient to her husband, good, helps the needy and fears the Lord, trustworthy, not idle, wears modest apparel, and learns in quietness without having authority over or teaching men. *That's not all,* he thought. *What else?* Quickly he remembered the others: not a busybody or tattler, and one who is not contentious. *Those are important ones to remember, too!* he thought. He was reminded that courtship was going to be a fun time, an exciting time, but also a time of hard work, observing, thought, and prayer. *I can only do it with Your help, Lord,* he prayed.

As he turned onto the state highway, he had another thought. *She's going to be observing me, also.* That thought sobered him somewhat. He remembered the traits that Dad had talked about in a godly man.  Would he display them?  Which areas did he still need work on?  Would those cause Jenny not to want to marry him?  It was definitely sobering. *Help me to be myself and answer honestly*, he prayed. *I want her to learn who I really am, not someone that I might pretend to be.*  Jeff remembered the lesson he had learned from the encounters with Lisa.

Pulling into Jenny's driveway, Jeff took a deep breath and walked to the front door.  Although he realized that their meetings would be serious, the Lord gave him a lightness of heart again as he rang the doorbell. *Still, this is fun*, he thought.

Ten-year-old Amy answered the door.  "Hello, Mr. McLean," Amy said.

Jeff almost turned around to see if Dad was standing behind him, then realized that Amy was addressing him.  "Hi, Amy," Jeff replied.  "You can just call me Jeff," he added, smiling.

Amy didn't respond.  She just grinned and ran out of the room.  "Mr. . . . I mean, Jeff is here," she shouted.

Ruth Barker, Jenny's mother, walked into the living room.  "Hello, Jeff.  Welcome.  Can I take your hat?  Would you like to have a seat?  I'm afraid most people are busy in the kitchen right now, trying to get everything finished.  Dinner should be ready soon."

Jeff handed Mrs. Barker his hat and sat down in the recliner beside the fireplace.

"Mr. Barker should be home before too long," she said.  "He had to work late tonight.  He's an accountant, as you know, and they are finishing a big audit. The final report is due in a few days and they're working hard to meet the deadline."

# Jeff McLean: His Courtship

"That's okay," Jeff said. "There are days and times of the year that we are extra busy on the farm, and it would be hard to catch us. Unless you were willing to hop on a tractor." Jeff and Mrs. Barker talked about his life on the farm.

In a few moments, Amy walked back into the room. "Supper is about ready," she said. "Should we go ahead and put it in the serving pieces or wait until Dad comes home?"

"Let's just wait . . . No, I think that's him I hear now," Mrs. Barker said. Looking out of the window, she continued, "Yes, there he is now. You can go ahead and put it all on the table. We can eat as soon as Dad gets washed up."

Soon everyone was seated at the table. Mr. Barker prayed, then the food was passed around the table. Jeff took very small helpings, not wanting to appear greedy or too hungry. Mrs. Barker noticed the size of his helpings.

"Jeff, you go ahead and spoon out as much as you want," she said. "Don't be bashful. We cooked a lot. I know that it takes a lot of food for a hard-working man like you."

Jeff blushed a little and looked around the table. So, it was obvious that he was acting a little differently than he normally would. *And I said I was going to be myself!* he thought. *Help me Lord Jesus to be myself!*

From then on, Jeff took out his normal-sized helpings. That doesn't mean that he was piggish in any way. There was plenty of food on the table. In fact, it looked to Jeff like they had planned on a dinner party of twenty or so!

"So, you're here to court Jenny," Ricky, Jenny's

little four-year-old brother, blurted out.

"Ricky!" Mrs. Barker implored.

"Yes, I am," Jeff answered without embarrassment.  "That is if it's okay with you, Ricky?"

"I like you," Ricky admitted.  "You drive a tractor."

"It's nice to have an insider on your side," Jeff remarked.  Everyone laughed.

So, the topic had been broached.  Somehow Ricky's comment broke the ice and allowed everyone to be a little more free and open in their conversation.  Everyone was more relaxed, even in the way they were sitting.

Still, the topics at the table centered on general things happening in their community and on people they all knew from church.  *We're going to have to get deeper than this*, Jeff thought.  *But I suppose there is plenty of time.  We can't be in a hurry.*

After supper, Mrs. Barker and Amy worked on the dishes, while everyone else moved to the living room.  As the conversation continued, Jeff noticed that Jenny was quiet in the way she spoke.  He also noticed that she seemed to love Ricky very much.  That was good, since it provided some evidence that she loved children.

Mr. Barker talked for a while about his job and the extra busy times of the year for him.  "Tax season, from January 1 to April 15, is the busiest.  Everyone knows to let me sleep late on April 16," he laughed.  "I usually plan a vacation for the end of April, so that everyone can have a lot of time with me.  I'm not complaining, though.  My job has been good for me.  It has helped me provide for my family."

# Jeff McLean:  His Courtship

After a pause, Mr. Barker continued.  "Farming has worked well for your father.  As a way to provide for his family, I mean.  I assume you think it's going to provide a reasonable income for you, too?" he asked.

"I'm counting on it," Jeff answered honestly.  "I never expect to get rich, yet I don't think I'll go hungry either."

"What about all the farmers we hear about going bankrupt?" Mr. Barker questioned.  This was obviously a concern for him.

*Is Jenny worried about that also?* Jeff wondered.

"Many farmers do go bankrupt," Jeff admitted.  "I can't promise that I won't.  No one can promise that, I don't suppose," he said wisely.  "Yet, if you look at many of those instances, it's because the man is heavily in debt and can't make his payments.  Then he has no option but to go bankrupt."

Jeff paused a moment, then slowly continued.  "I know there have been a few hard times for my dad.  But because he doesn't believe in going into debt, those times were manageable.  I feel the same way he does about debt."

With that, Mr. Barker changed the subject and started asking about Jeff's life on the farm.  Everyone was interested.  Ricky seemed to be sitting on the edge of his seat, and Jeff knew he had Jenny's undivided attention as well.

Jeff was telling a funny story about what happened once when he had forgotten to unhitch the haybine, when Mrs. Barker called from the kitchen, "Jenny, can you come here please?"  Jenny didn't ask if she could wait a minute and hear the ending of the story.  And, she didn't "drag her feet" as she was leaving so that she could hear the story. Instead, she immediately stood up and walked out of the room. That impressed Jeff. *Obedient,* he thought. *And not self-willed. Those are good traits to have!*

As the evening came to an end, Jeff addressed Mr. and Mrs. Barker. "Thank you for having me here tonight. I've really enjoyed myself." Looking directly at Jenny, he repeated, "I really have."

"We've enjoyed having you," Jenny said softly. "Please come again."

"I will," Jeff promised. "Good night."

Over the next several weeks, Jeff and Jenny had the opportunity to visit with each other a number of times. Sometimes it was at Jeff's parents' home, and at other times it was at the Barkers' home. During one devotion time at the Barker home, Jeff got to hear Jenny pray specifically for their courtship. "Dear Father, thank you that you are allowing me to get to know Jeff," she prayed. "You know that we want Your will to be done, not ours. Please give us wisdom and discernment. Please take away the sins of my life and make me the woman you want me to be. Help me not to covet what others have but be grateful for Your provision. Forgive me for the impatience I had with Mom today about the supper. Help me to learn more patience and kindness . . ."

The more Jeff saw, the more he realized that God had prepared Jenny to be a godly wife for someone. She was naturally friendly, and Jeff could see that she was someone he could easily become best friends with. She didn't push her opinions on him. Instead, she was content to listen to Jeff's ideas and then voice hers when asked. That didn't mean that she had no opinions or that she wasn't carefully examining Jeff to see if he was the man she wanted to marry.  It simply reflected her self-control and desire to be meek and gentle.

A good example of this was when Jeff asked Jenny what kind of furnishings she liked most.  "What do you mean by furnishings?" Jenny asked.

"You know.  Tables, lamps, chairs, things on the wall," Jeff tried to explain.  "I know that some women like fancy, new things while others seem to be happy even if the furnishings aren't new.  Also, some like modern things while others I know seem to like plain, old-fashioned things.  How about you?"

"Is there some type that you like best?" she asked.

"Maybe," Jeff hedged.  "But I'd like to know what you like first."

Jenny laughed.  "I suppose if I had to give my opinion, I would say that I like some of both.  I like new china and new silverware.  I guess I don't like the thought of eating off of plates and using silverware that someone else has used.  I also like the new kinds of linens and drapes that are in fashion now.  On the other hand, I do like the look and feel of real wood, not imitation wood, in furniture.  To be honest with you, though, I could be perfectly happy with whatever furnishings I had."

So, Jeff was encouraged with what he was seeing in Jenny.  She wasn't perfect.  He had noticed that she could get frustrated with Ricky at times.  He had also noticed that she sometimes corrected her parents or siblings even when it really wasn't necessary.  He had questions as to whether she would be able to handle the stress and strain of hard work that a farmer's wife

# Jeff McLean: His Courtship

often has to endure. So, he needed more time to observe and talk with Jenny. Even so, Jeff could feel God blessing their time together. Mom and Dad had mostly good comments about Jenny, too.

*I wonder what she thinks of me?* he asked himself one evening after Jenny left. *She's so quiet that I can't really tell what she thinks about what she sees in me.* He hoped to get a better feel for that during their next visit together.

# Chapter Sixteen

J enny visited at the McLean home the following week on a rainy Tuesday.  It was the busy time of putting up peaches.  Mom always bought five bushels of fresh peaches and for several days, the sweet smell of peaches being cut up and canned filled the house. It was hot, messy work over the canners of boiling water all day.  Yet, it was worth the effort to see the rows and rows of canned peaches on the storage shelves in the basement.  Jenny volunteered to help, and everyone in the family participated except Dad.

"These are really good peaches," Jenny commented, eating a slice.  "Where do you buy them?"

"Thanks," Mom replied.  "They're later than usual this year but we are always grateful to get them.  We have a friend who goes upstate a ways and buys them by the truckload.  We call her the 'fruit lady.'  She finds the best prices and the best fruit and then resells them to a number of families in the area."

"That sounds like a good way to do things," Jenny said.  "Mmm, I don't think I've ever had any peaches that tasted this good!"

"Here, I'll clean away your scraps," Becky offered kindly, dropping peach skins and seeds into a bucket. "Do you put up peaches at your house?"

"No, we don't anymore," Jenny said.  "We haven't done any canning for years at our house.  You see, I got really sick with pneumonia one summer about five years ago.  No, it was six.  Anyway, it was a pretty

# Jeff McLean:  His Courtship

bad case and it came on about the time that Mom was canning some corn.  Mom was afraid that if she filled the house with all of that steam, it would hurt me. We've since learned that moisture in the air can actually help someone with pneumonia.  I guess she never decided to start canning again."

"I got pneumonia once," Steve said, dropping another cut peach into the big bowl in the center of the table.  "That was no fun!"

"I suppose you have to take it easy somewhat," Jeff asked.  "I mean, since you had pneumonia, do you have to take precautions?  Are your lungs weaker?"

Jenny reached down and picked up several more peaches from a basket.  "The doctors said that my pneumonia shouldn't cause me any further trouble at all.  But, to be honest with you, I don't feel like I have the energy to do what I used to do.  Maybe it's not energy that I mean.  I guess it's mostly in the winter that I sometimes have a little trouble.  On a really cold day, it seems more difficult to breathe than it once did. It could just be my imagination, though."

"That's too bad," Jeff said.  "I got frostbite a few winters ago, and I've noticed that the extreme cold affects me more than it used to.  I don't get short of breath, or anything like that.  It just hurts my face and hands."

"Have you thought of moving further south?" Jenny asked.  "I've often wondered if that might help me some in the winter.  It might not, though.  I just wonder sometimes if it would."

Jeff had never considered moving south. This was where his family lived, and where he wanted to live. *Would she be unhappy living up here the rest of her*

# Jeff McLean: His Courtship

*life?* he asked himself. Then, answering, he said, "No, I don't think I could move away from this part of the country. Unless God was leading me somewhere else, of course." *Or unless my wife's health required it,* he thought to himself.

Jenny didn't say anything. She just kept cutting up peaches and placing them in the large stainless steel bowl in the center of the table.

"Ow!" Rachel exclaimed. "Cut myself again! I must learn to be more careful. Mom, can I go sit with Samuel out on the porch for a while? It would give my cuts a chance to heal."

"Of course," Mom said kindly, as she placed more empty jars into the canner to get sterilized. "Can I get you a Band-Aid®?"

"No thanks," Rachel answered. "I've rinsed it off. I just want to make sure it stops bleeding before I start cutting peaches again. That will probably help the taste of our peaches, too."

Everyone laughed.

"I suppose you know Mrs. Kyle, your neighbor, pretty well, don't you?" Janet asked.

"Yes," Jenny answered. "She and I have become good friends. I enjoy babysitting her little boys some-times."

"Well, I heard that she was thinking about selling all of her goats. Has she said anything to you about it?" Janet wondered.

Jenny was silent for a moment. She chose her words carefully. "If I've heard anything about that, I'm afraid I couldn't say." Then, trying to change the subject, she began to talk about the little Kyle twin boys and how much fun it was to dress them in match-

# Jeff McLean: His Courtship

ing clothes.

After a while, Mom dismissed most of her helpers except for Becky and Rachel. "You all have gotten way ahead of me and this canner," Mom said. "Take a break and we can do more after lunch." Jeff and Jenny went to the back porch to rest.

"What do you think about this family of mine?" Jeff asked, laughing. "Think you could stand to be around them the rest of your life?" It wasn't exactly what he had intended to say, but it just sort of fell out of his mouth. He had hoped to learn something about her interest in him as a possible mate. She was so quiet, that it was hard sometimes to know what she was thinking.

"I like your family very much," she replied honestly. "Yes, it would fun to be around them, watching them grow up," she said a little shyly.

About that time, Samuel came around the corner. He was wearing bright yellow rubber boots and was holding a large red golf umbrella. Walking up to Jenny, he imparted some very important news to her.

"Jenny, see that bird feeder over there?" he asked, pointing toward a tree near the house. "Well, if you see a bird with long hair down its back," he said, "that's a *girl* one." With that he raced back around the side of the house.

Jeff and Jenny both laughed. "Yes, your family is fun," she repeated.

The two sat there enjoying the sound of rain gently pattering on the porch roof. "Jeff, I know you've been a Christian for a number of years," Jenny began. "I noticed a long time ago that you seemed to be a good boy, and now you seem to me to be a good man." She stopped.

*I wonder what she's going to ask?* Jeff wondered. He began to try to think of where this conversation was heading. Finally, he tried to encourage her to continue by saying, "Yes?"

"One thing that I think is important," she began again, slowly, "is that the man should be able to teach spiritual things to his wife and children. I don't know how to ask it. And I don't know if you would know or not. But, I'll ask it anyway. Do you think you would be a good teacher?"

Jeff was caught a little off-guard. "I pray that I would be," he answered honestly. "Of course, I've not had a chance to do it, really. There have been times when one of my younger brothers or sisters has asked me a question and I've tried to answer it for them. I can't say how good I was, though. I guess you would have to ask them that question."

Both were silent for a time. "There are many traits that a husband and wife are supposed to have," Jenny said, "that are a little hard to assess before a person actually becomes a husband or a wife. Don't you think so?"

"Yes," Jeff responded. "I suppose we can only use the evidence that we have at the time, along with the discernment of our parents and the Holy Spirit, of course."

"That's true," Jenny agreed. "We do have the Holy Spirit as a guide and counselor."

"Jenny, is there anything about me that concerns you?" Jeff asked suddenly. "I mean, I know I'm not perfect. I'm just wondering which of my imperfect traits you've noticed the most."

# Jeff McLean: His Courtship

Jenny smiled at the way Jeff phrased it. Yet, inside she prayed, *Help me Lord to be honest and gentle.* "Well, one thing I've noticed sometimes is that you compare me to your older sister, Sarah. I know that would be natural for you, since I've learned how close you two are. And I think it's great that you two love each other so much. Yet, I'm not Sarah. I never will be. I guess I'm afraid that even after we were married you might continue to compare me to Sarah, or to your mom. And I know I won't measure up to either of them in many ways. That concerns me."

Jeff was silent. He had known for some time that he was guilty of doing that, yet didn't think it showed. Now he knew. "Jenny, you're right. I'm sorry. Please forgive me. And I will try to do better, I promise. I think God has blessed me with a wonderful mom and great brothers and sisters. And you're right. Sarah has always been special to me. Even though she's married and moved away I still consider her to be my best friend. I would want my wife to be my best friend and would do everything I could to make sure that happened. It wouldn't happen overnight, but I hope you believe me when I say that is what I seriously want my wife to become."

"I believe you," Jenny said softly. "That's the kind of relationship I am looking for in a husband, too."

The two continued to talk for a long time. Their conversation covered a wide range of topics, some serious, and some not so serious. After a while, Mom called everyone in to get washed up for lunch.

After the blessing, everyone made themselves a sandwich from among the items spread out on the kitchen counter. Although they had tried to clean up

# Jeff McLean: His Courtship

the kitchen somewhat, there was still sticky peach juice on the floor. Naturally, Samuel stepped right into a big spot. "Mom, my sock is all wet with peach juice!" Samuel exclaimed, beginning to have tears in his eyes.

"Well, I don't think it's going to do any permanent damage to you," Mom answered, smiling. "Becky, can you run and get him some more socks? And Rachel, would you please finish cleaning that little spot of juice that we must have missed. . . No, don't use Samuel's sock. Please use a wet paper towel."

Everyone was finally seated. Actually, that's not exactly true. It seemed like someone was always jumping up to get first this, then that. As Mom was finally sitting down to eat her sandwich, Steve and Ben were already going back for their second ones.

The lunch conversation centered around the weather. "Has anyone listened to the weather radio since breakfast?" Dad asked. He had some hay down, and wondered if the sun might pop out later in the day.

"It's supposed to start clearing this afternoon with winds out of the south at 15 miles per hour," Mom answered.

"I heard the radio when you had it on, Mrs. McLean, " Jenny offered, helpfully. "Actually, they said it is supposed to be 15 to 20 miles per hour." No one said anything.

Dad said that it would still probably be several days before the hay would dry. Talk then centered on what the family would be doing for the rest of the day. "Peaches!" Mom said, cheerily. "Most of us are going to be doing more peaches!"

After lunch, while Rachel and Janet were clearing

# Jeff McLean: His Courtship

away the lunch dishes, Jeff and Jenny returned to the porch. Earlier in the day, Dad had instructed Jeff to just spend some time with Jenny, since there was nothing urgent that needed Jeff's help.

"Your mom is a very hard worker," Jenny commented. "To can all morning, then prepare lunch, then to get back to it right away. I'm impressed with her energy. I'm afraid I would never be able to do half of what your mom gets done every day."

"God has blessed her with energy," Jeff agreed. He had always thought that all moms were probably just like his mom until he had started visiting in his friends' homes. Some women just didn't seem to be able to get much done.

"Jenny, I know I'm not your husband and don't have authority over you, but there's something that's bothering me that I feel I should bring up," Jeff said, changing the subject suddenly. "It may not be a big deal, but I want to talk about it anyway."

Jeff didn't know how to begin. *Just jump in and say it*, he decided. "I know that sometimes it is important to correct someone when they say something that isn't true. For instance, if I'm adding a chemical to a tank and the directions say to add one quart. If I misread it and think it's supposed to be one gallon, that's something that is worthy of a correction." He paused, less confident that he had a right to even be saying this to Jenny.

"Go on," Jenny encouraged.

"It's just how you corrected Mom at lunchtime. You know, when you said that she was wrong about the wind speed. I guess I don't feel that was important enough to warrant a correction." When she didn't respond, he added, "I hope I haven't said this in an unkind way."

She didn't say anything.

"Do you know what I'm talking about?  In our house, Dad has taught us that we shouldn't correct each other on minor points.  If someone is telling a story and they get a little point mixed up or give the wrong date, we've been taught not to correct them. Dad says that a correcting spirit can lead to an arguing spirit.  I think that's true, also."

"I'm sorry," Jenny answered.  "No one has ever said anything about that to me before.  I didn't realize that correcting a mistake could concern anyone."

Jeff tried to think of what to say next.  "Well, let me ask you.  How do you feel when you're telling a story and someone interrupts you and corrects you on a minor point?  Then after you tell a little more, they interrupt you again and correct another minor point? Has that ever happened to you?  How did you feel?"

Putting it in those terms helped Jenny suddenly realize the problem that Jeff saw in such behavior.  "I don't like it," she finally admitted.  "You're right.  I guess I've just gotten in the habit of listening for tiny details and correcting if someone is wrong.  Maybe I do it because that is what my parents and other people do too.  If I correct others, then I don't feel so stupid when they are correcting me.  I guess it's just pride, isn't it?"

"It probably is," Jeff replied gently.  "I deal with pride also," he admitted.  "Yet, we need to remove it when we find it."

"I'll try to do better," she promised.  After a second, she added, "And not just when *you* are

# Jeff McLean: His Courtship

around, either. I think you're right. Thanks for sharing that with me."

*She's teachable!* Jeff shouted to himself. *Hooray!*

# Chapter Seventeen

In several other small issues that were discussed in the next couple of months, Jeff continued to notice how teachable Jenny was.  She didn't take offence when he brought forth several issues to discuss.  Yet, she did hold a firm belief in what she knew was right, so she wasn't just someone who went along with whatever anyone told her.

"Can we visit your farm, soon?" she asked Jeff during a visit to the McLeans.  "I would like to see what you've done there and get some idea about your plans for the place."

Jeff was a little hesitant to take her.   The court-ship seemed to be going so smoothly, and this was the area that he was most concerned about.  The house wasn't fixed up at all inside.  In fact, because it hadn't really been cleaned in a while, it looked worse than it did when Mrs. Walters moved out.  He also remem-bered Lisa's reaction and didn't want a repeat of that experience.  Yet, she certainly did have a right to see it. *What am I doing, trying to hide something again?* he asked himself. *I promised to be open and honest in all my dealings.*

"Sure, we can take a look at it.  Let me see if Mom and Dad would like to go along also."  Secretly, he hoped that Mom might be able to help Jenny see the potential in the house if that became necessary.

Soon all four were standing in Jeff's driveway. Jeff pointed out the buildings, and how he thought the farm would look in a few years.  "Let's look at the

# Jeff McLean: His Courtship

barn first," he suggested.

Jenny seemed impressed with it. "It's old, in a neat kind of way," she said. "I can imagine a farmer having cows here, back when times were simpler and life was slower. Perhaps whoever lives here can keep that idea alive somehow, just by recognizing that we don't have to rush around at breakneck speed everywhere."

"I like that," Dad said. "That's a good thought. Almost all of us could stand to slow down some."

Jenny looked toward the house. "Shall we see it next?" she asked.

Jeff had hoped to show her the beautiful pastures and hay fields first. Then, maybe she wouldn't be so disappointed in the house. *There I go again*, he scolded himself. "Sure, let's go and take a look." He decided not to even warn her what kind of condition it was in before they entered the house.

The house had a stale odor that comes from not opening windows for long periods of time. Jeff noticed spider webs and dust that he hadn't really noticed just a few days ago. He started to apologize, but stopped himself. *Let her see it for what it is today*, he thought. *If she sees potential in it, then there is more than room for hope!*

Slowly, she walked through all of the rooms of the house. She even opened every closet and looked inside. After touring the upstairs, she walked back down to the kitchen and pointed to a door. "I guess that must be the way to the cellar?"

"Yes," Jeff answered. "There's a light switch just inside the door. But please be careful, the stairs are a little loose." So far, Jenny hadn't made any comment.

# Jeff McLean: His Courtship

The basement seemed a little more musty than Jeff had remembered.

Jenny was moving over to where the washer and dryer hookups were. "I guess this is where most of the . . ." She didn't finish her sentence because just at that moment, she ran into a huge spider web draped across the room. Since she was talking when she ran into it, some of it got stuck in her mouth.

"Uhhhh!" she exclaimed. "I have never liked spiders!" Quickly she removed the filaments from her mouth and hair. "Did I get it all out of my hair?" Jenny anxiously asked Mom. "Is there any on my dress?"

Mom picked off some threads from Jenny's dress. "I think that about gets it all."

"I don't suppose you can get away from spiders. As I was saying," Jenny continued, "I guess this is where most of the laundry gets cleaned. Which makes sense, since people with muddy or manure-covered clothes would come straight here and change. Isn't that the way it would work?"

"That's the way it should work," Dad answered her with a smile. "Unless the man sometimes forgets and runs upstairs still dirty. I think I've heard of that happening a time or two to someone I know."

Mom hugged Dad. "That's okay," she assured him. "I still love you. Even if you do ruin my clean floors sometimes."

After looking over the cellar, Jenny led the way back out of the house. *What do you think about it?* Jeff wanted to shout. The suspense was almost more than he could bear.

"Jeff has a nice place, don't you think?" Dad said

# Jeff McLean: His Courtship

to Jenny. "There's real potential here."

"I was just thinking the same thing," Jenny remarked. "Of course, the house needs a woman's touch here and there, and a good cleaning, but it does seem to have potential." After turning and looking at the entire farm, she continued. "I agree with you, Jeff. God has really blessed you with this place."

"Did you see the flower beds?" Jeff asked. "I'm afraid it's too late in the year for you to see the actual flowers."

"Yes, I did. I'm sure they're beautiful," Jenny answered. "I'm afraid I've never worked with flowers or shrubs much at all. I'm not against learning. It's just that I have never done much with them. Do you enjoy working with flowers?"

"I enjoy looking at them," was Jeff's honest reply. "I've never really worked much with them myself."

Upon reaching the McLeans' house, Mom offered everyone some cool lemonade. "This should taste good about now," she remarked. The other McLean children gathered around the porch, as Dad told some funny incidents that had occurred when he put up hay as a young man.

Before Jenny left, she asked Jeff, "Do you think I could come over sometime when you're working on your farm and help? I may be in the way, but I would at least like to see what it would be like. I've never done anything like that before."

Jeff was thrilled. "Sure, I was planning on working over there on Friday. Janet and Ben were going to help me knock some old plaster off the walls in the kitchen. It will be hard work, but you're sure welcome to come."

# Jeff McLean: His Courtship

"I'll see you on Friday," Jenny promised as she turned and walked down the driveway.

"Imagine that!" Jeff said, smiling as he walked away. "Imagine that!"

On Friday, Jenny was true to her word. Apparently she was serious about working, because she showed up in an old dress that Jeff had never seen before. She even had on a pair of gardening gloves. "I didn't bring a hammer or anything, although Dad said that is what I would probably be using. I assume you have one I can borrow."

"Sure," Jeff grinned. Before long, the plaster was crashing to the floor and the air was filled with plaster dust. The noise was almost deafening as four hammers pounded on the walls. Jeff looked over at Jenny, concerned not only for her safety, but also worried that the dust might bother her lungs. She had tied a long scarf over her mouth and nose, but still she was coughing.

After a while, he walked over to her. "Let's go out and get some fresh air," he suggested. "Whatever you say," she replied. Soon all four workers were in the fresh air.

"What a lot of dust!" Ben commented, blowing his nose. "Is it always that dusty, Jeff?"

"Usually is," Jeff said. "Are you all right, Jenny?" Jenny was still coughing.

In a moment, she was able to stop coughing enough to answer. "I'm okay. Just can't seem to stop coughing."

Jeff offered her a cup of water. He informed Jenny that he thought it best for her not to continue tearing out the old plaster. "I'm sorry I can't do what needs to be done," she said in a disappointed voice. "I tried, though."

"That's okay," Jeff said. He was thankful for what he had seen in the last thirty minutes. Jenny had tried to work hard and hadn't complained. She also seemed to have been willing to continue the work if Jeff had allowed it. Yet, when he told her to stop, she accepted his authority to do so without an argument. That spoke volumes to Jeff.

"Is there anything else I can do?" Jenny asked. "I'm okay, really."

Jeff thought for a moment. "Maybe you would like to tear off some of the siding on the back porch instead? It won't cause any dust and the air out here is fine." Jenny was happy for the chance to continue doing something at the farm.

Jeff checked on her from time to time. She didn't really know how to efficiently use the wrecking bar that Jeff had given her, but she was trying as hard as she could. In fact, he was surprised at the progress she had made once when he checked on her.

"That's great!" he praised. "You've gotten a lot done since I was here the last time."

Jenny laughed. "My wrecking bar was caught in two long boards. When I started pulling hard, I sort of fell off the ladder. The boards came down with me!" At Jeff's concerned expression, she put him at ease. "Don't worry. I didn't get hurt. I've just been trying to decide if maybe I should start falling off the ladder more often. I'd get a lot more done that way!"

Although she worked as hard as she could, Jenny didn't have the stamina that Ben or Janet had. She

# Jeff McLean: His Courtship

had to take more frequent breaks and was ready for lunch long before anyone else even began to think about it. Heading to Dad's farm, she confessed, "I'm sorry I wasn't much help. I'm not used to that much physical work at one time."

"Don't you worry about it for a second," Jeff beamed. "You did fine. Thanks for your help. And even more, thanks for your desire to help." The two were silent the rest of the way to the farm.

After lunch, Jenny had to leave. "Thanks again for your help," Jeff repeated. "I hope to see you again soon."

# Chapter Eighteen

Jeff sat in the barn loft, thinking about Jenny. He pulled out a small plastic case that held little pieces of paper the size of a business card. The pieces of paper had Bible verses on them that Jeff was trying to memorize. The last card was a list of the important traits of a Godly woman. Jeff had made this card after his dad's teaching and had memorized them long ago. Still he pulled the card out and scanned the list once more. After reading each trait he would pause, and look up at the barn roof, thinking. He thought about the conversations and meetings he had with Jenny. *She has so many on the list already, and seems to be working on the rest*, he concluded.

Jeff stood and stretched his legs. Moving to the open door, he looked out over the brown hay fields. He began to think about the many conversations he had with his mom and dad concerning Jenny. They had provided counsel and comments all along the way. They had even pointed out areas that he and Jenny should discuss further. Because of their wise counsel and aid, Jeff felt like he knew more about Jenny than most men knew about their brides.

"Dear Heavenly Father," he prayed quietly, "thank You that You and Your Word have been my primary guides throughout this process. Thank You for parents that have desired the best for me and that have shown me many things that You desired them to show me. Thank You that You have brought Jenny into my life, and that You have given me a peace about her.

# Jeff McLean: His Courtship

Help Your will to be done in everything. Help me not to fear, but to trust in You. May I be the godly man that You desire me to be. In Jesus' Name, amen." With that he walked toward the ladder which led to the lower part of the barn. Communion with God, through prayer and Bible study, had been Jeff's constant companion throughout the entire courtship process.

Jeff approached his dad and mom who were in the kitchen. "For the past several months, I've been praying for God's guidance," he began. "And I've been observing Jenny and asking her questions. Dad, I think I am ready to ask her to marry me."

Dad came over and slapped his back. "We've been praying and observing also," he said. "Your mom and I have already agreed that she would make a fine wife for you. We give you our permission *and* blessing to marry Jenny."

"Thanks, Dad. Thanks, Mom," Jeff said, hugging his parents. "I'm going to talk with her father tomorrow then, if that is all right with you."

"I look forward to hearing your report about that conversation," Dad replied happily. "We'll pray that God's will would be done."

"I would like to marry your daughter," Jeff began, when Mr. Barker was seated in his easy chair. "I've prayed about it and my parents have prayed about it. We have all come to the conclusion that this is the right direction I should take."

Mr. Barker was happy. He liked Jeff a lot. Over the last months, he had gotten to know Jeff even better, and was impressed with what he saw. In their

# Jeff McLean: His Courtship

conversations, he had almost marveled at Jeff's mature answers to his questions. Still, this was his oldest child, and the first one to go through a courtship. He was learning and certainly didn't want to make any mistakes.

He knew that Jeff wasn't perfect and that Jenny would face a number of challenges as his wife. Jenny would have to get used to the rigors of living on a farm, something that he knew would be a strain at times. Also, Jenny had often expressed an interest in moving to the South. That wasn't going to happen with Jeff. And then there were the areas in which Jeff just needed more time in which to mature. Thankfully, Jeff was truly interested in maturing and being sanctified by the Holy Spirit.

"That's good news, Jeff," he replied finally. "As you can imagine, I would like to spend a bit more time praying about this and seeking counsel. I'll let you know soon, okay?"

Jeff only wanted God's will for his life. If that meant waiting a while for everyone to feel comfortable about him asking Jenny, that was okay with him. *After all*, he thought. *I'll be married for years and years, God willing. What's a few more days to wait to know?*

Toward the end of the week, Jeff noticed Mr. Barker pulling into the McLean driveway. *Well, I guess it's time to find out*, he thought. Walking quickly up to Mr. Barker, he held out his hand, "Good morning, Mr. Barker."

"Good morning, Jeff," Mr. Barker returned. "I have some good news for you. It is with pleasure that

# Jeff McLean: His Courtship

I encourage you to ask my daughter to marry you."
He said a few other things, but truthfully Jeff didn't
hear them. Jeff was just trying to decide when he
could go and talk to Jenny.

"So, that's the way we will leave it, then," Mr.
Barker finished.

*Leave what?* thought Jeff. *I should have been
listening!* "Sir?" he had to ask Mr. Barker.

Mr. Barker just laughed. He had noticed Jeff's
excitement and difficulty in attending to the conversation. "I just said that you can ask Jenny whenever you
think it is best. I've not told her of our conversation,
but I did tell her that her mother and I are in agreement that we give her our blessing if you should ask
her."

"Is she home right now?" asked Jeff.

"She was when I left," Mr. Barker replied with a
smile.

"Thanks," Jeff said. He then turned and walked
quickly toward the barn. "Dad, I'm going to be gone
for a while," he stated.

"Doesn't have anything to do with Mr. Barker
standing in our driveway, does it?"

Jeff turned to look. *I didn't even say good bye or
anything,* he thought. *I just walked off and left him
standing there. I've got to get a hold of myself.* Then
addressing his dad, he answered, "Yes, they have
given their blessing to my asking Jenny to marry me.
And she's home right now!"

"Imagine that!" Dad exclaimed, trying to pretend
to sound shocked. "Well, I hope you're on your way
there."

"Yes sir," Jeff assured him. "See you later!"

# Jeff McLean: His Courtship

Within twenty minutes, Jeff walked into the Barker's living room with Jenny. She motioned to the couch and they both sat down. As soon as she was seated, she could tell he was excited about something because he kept pulling at a thread that wasn't really loose on his jeans. "You certainly seem happy today," she commented, laughing.

"I am," he said. "I just had a talk with your dad." He couldn't hold it back. "Jenny, will you do me the honor of becoming Mrs. Jeff McLean?"

Jenny blushed, then looked straight into Jeff's eyes in a way she had never done before. "Mrs. Jeff McLean. Mrs. Jeff McLean," she repeated, slowly. "I like that. Yes, I like that very much. Even more I like what it means." Then lowering her voice, she answered quietly, "Yes."

The End

Please read "A Note From the Authors" in the front of this book if you haven't already.

# Castleberry Farms Press

Our primary goal in publishing is to provide wholesome books in a manner that brings honor to our Lord. We believe in setting no evil thing before our eyes (Psalm 101:3) and although there are many outstanding books, we have had trouble finding enough good reading material for our children. Therefore, we feel the Lord has led us to start this family business.

We believe the following: The Bible is the infallible true Word of God. That God is the Creator and Controller of the universe. That Jesus Christ is the only begotten Son of God, born of the virgin Mary, lived a perfect life, was crucified, buried, rose again, sits at the right hand of God, and makes intercession for the saints. That Jesus Christ is the only Savior and way to the Father. That salvation is based on faith alone, but true faith will produce good works. That the Holy Spirit is given to believers as Guide and Comforter. That the Lord Jesus will return again. That man was created to glorify God and enjoy Him forever.

We began writing and publishing in mid-1996 and hope to add more books in the future if the Lord is willing. All books are written by Mr. and Mrs. Castleberry.

We would love to hear from you if you have any comments or suggestions. Our address is at the end of this section. Now, we'll tell you a little about our books.

# The Courtship Series

These books are written to encourage those who intend to follow a Biblically-based courtship that includes the active involvement of parents. The main characters are committed followers of Jesus Christ, and Christian family values are emphasized throughout. The reader will be encouraged to heed parental advice and to live in obedience to the Lord.

## *Jeff McLean: His Courtship*

Follow the story of Jeff McLean as he seeks God's direction for his life. This book is the newest in our courtship series, and is written from a young man's perspective. A discussion of godly traits to seek in young men and women is included as part of the story. February 1998. ISBN 1-891907-05-0. Paperback. $7.50 (plus shipping and handling).

## *The Courtship of Sarah McLean*

Sarah McLean is a nineteen year-old girl who longs to become a wife and mother. The book chronicles a period of two years, in which she has to learn to trust her parents and God fully in their decisions for her future. Paperback, 2nd printing, 1997. ISBN 1-891907-00-X. $7.50 (plus shipping and handling).

## *Waiting for Her Isaac*

Sixteen year-old Beth Grant is quite happy with her life and has no desire for any changes. But God has many lessons in store before she is ready for courtship. The story of Beth's spiritual journey toward godly womanhood is told along with the story of her courtship. Paperback. 1997. ISBN 1-891907-03-4. $7.50 (plus shipping and handling).

# The Farm Mystery Series

Join Jason and Andy as they try to solve the mysterious happenings on the Nelson family's farm. These are books that the whole family will enjoy. In fact, many have used them as read-aloud-to-the-family books. Parents can be assured that there are no murders or other objectionable elements in these books. The boys learn lessons in obedience and responsibility while having lots of fun. There are no worldly situations or language, and no boy-girl relationships. Just happy and wholesome Christian family life, with lots of everyday adventure woven in.

## *Footprints in the Barn*

Who is the man in the green car? What is going on in the hayloft? Is there something wrong with the mailbox? And what's for lunch? The answers to these and many other interesting questions are found in the book Footprints in the Barn. Hardcover. 1996. ISBN 1-891907-01-8. $12 (plus shipping and handling).

### The Mysterious Message

The Great Detective Agency is at it once again, solving mysteries on the Nelson farmstead. Why is there a pile of rocks in the woods? Is someone stealing gas from the mill? How could a railroad disappear? And will Jason and Andy have to eat biscuits without honey? You will have to read this second book in the Farm Mystery Series to find out. Paperback. 1997. ISBN 1-891907-04-2. $7.50 (plus shipping and handling).

### Midnight Sky

What is that sound in the woods? Has someone been stealing Dad's tools? Why is a strange dog barking at midnight? And will the Nelsons be able to adopt Russian children? Midnight Sky provides the answers. Paperback. 1998. ISBN 1-891907-06-9. $7.50 (plus shipping and handling).

# Other Books

### Our Homestead Story: The First Years

The true and humorous account of one family's journey toward a more self-sufficient life-style with the help of God. Read about our experiences with cows, chickens, horses, sheep, gardening and more. Paperback. 1996. ISBN 1-891907-02-6. $7.50 (plus shipping and handling).

### *Call Her Blessed*

This book is designed to encourage mothers to consistently, day by day, follow God's will in their role as mothers. Examples are provided of mothers who know how to nurture and strengthen their children's faith in God. Paperback. 1998. ISBN 1-891907-08-5. $6.00 (plus shipping and handling).

### *The Orchard Lane Series:*
### *In the Spring of the Year*

Meet the Hunter family and share in their lives as they move to a new home. The first in our newest series, In the Spring of the Year is written especially for children ages 5-10. Nancy, Caleb, and Emily learn about obedience and self-denial while enjoying the simple pleasures of innocent childhood. Paperback. 1999. ISBN 1-891907-07-7. $8.00 (plus shipping and handling).

# Shipping and Handling Costs

The shipping and handling charge is $2.00 for the first book and 50¢ for each additional book you buy in the same order.

You can save on shipping by getting an order together with your friends or homeschool group. On orders of 10-24 books, shipping is only 50¢ per book. Orders of 25 or more books are shipped FREE. Just have each person write a check for their own total, send in all the checks, and indicate **one** address for shipping.

To order, please send a check for the total, including shipping (Wisconsin residents, please add 5.5% sales tax on the total, including shipping and handling charges) to:

Castleberry Farms Press
Dept. SY
P.O. Box 337
Poplar, WI 54864

**Please note that prices and shipping charges are subject to change.**

**CASTLEBERRY FARMS PRESS**
**P.O. BOX 337**
**POPLAR, WI 54864**

| Description | Quantity | Unit Price | Total |
|---|---|---|---|
| The Courtship of Sarah McLean | | $7.50 | |
| Waiting for Her Isaac | | $7.50 | |
| Jeff McLean: His Courtship | | $7.50 | |
| Footprints in the Barn (hardback) | | $12.00 | |
| The Mysterious Message | | $7.50 | |
| Midnight Sky | | $7.50 | |
| Our Homestead Story | | $7.50 | |
| Call Her Blessed | | $6.00 | |
| In the Spring of the Year | | $8.00 | |
| **Shipping and handling charge ($2.00 for first book, 50¢ for each additional)*** | | | |
| Wisconsin residents must add 5.5% sales tax (on total, including shipping costs) | | | |
| TOTAL DUE | | | |

Your name and address:

Note: If you know others who might like to have a catalog, please send us their names and addresses and we'll send them one. Thank you.

*Save on shipping! Get an order together with your friends or homeschool group. On orders of 10 or more books, shipping is only 50¢ per book. Orders of 25 or more books are shipped FREE. Just have each person write a check for their own total, send in all the checks, and indicate **one** address for shipping.

## CASTLEBERRY FARMS PRESS
## P.O. BOX 337
## POPLAR, WI 54864

| Description | Quantity | Unit Price | Total |
|---|---|---|---|
| The Courtship of Sarah McLean | | $7.50 | |
| Waiting for Her Isaac | | $7.50 | |
| Jeff McLean: His Courtship | | $7.50 | |
| Footprints in the Barn (hardback) | | $12.00 | |
| The Mysterious Message | | $7.50 | |
| Midnight Sky | | $7.50 | |
| Our Homestead Story | | $7.50 | |
| Call Her Blessed | | $6.00 | |
| In the Spring of the Year | | $8.00 | |
| **Shipping and handling charge ($2.00 for first book, 50¢ for each additional)*** | | | |
| Wisconsin residents must add 5.5% sales tax (on total, including shipping costs) | | | |
| TOTAL DUE | | | |

Your name and address:


Note: If you know others who might like to have a catalog, please send us their names and addresses and we'll send them one. Thank you.

*Save on shipping! Get an order together with your friends or homeschool group. On orders of 10 or more books, shipping is only 50¢ per book. Orders of 25 or more books are shipped FREE. Just have each person write a check for their own total, send in all the checks, and indicate **one** address for shipping.